LIBERTY BODICE
and
BLACK STOCKINGS

LIBERTY BODICE
and
BLACK STOCKINGS

MARIE STONE

Allison & Busby
Published by W.H. Allen & Co. Plc

An Allison & Busby book
Published in 1989 by
W.H. Allen & Co. Plc
Sekforde House
175/9 St John St
London EC1V 4LL

Copyright © 1986 by Marie Stone

Printed and bound in Great Britain by
Courier International Ltd, Tiptree, Essex

ISBN 0 7490 0020 1

Contents

LIBERTY BODICE

1

Please don't let me wet my knickers. She crossed her legs and the painful pleasant feeling, exacerbated by the cold, subsided. It was all right. She could hold it. There would be time.

She took the Bakelite eggcup from her satchel. Now for some water. The passages between the garages were wet but there was no water on the surface. It was no good: a christening had to be pure and clean to be right.

"I'll come back." The girl stretched up and kissed a supple single-limbed sycamore tree, growing from the mud behind the double-door pre-cast garage, the last in a line of eight that stepped up the hill. She hid the eggcup under her handkerchief and buckled up the leather strap. Her fingers were clumsy with cold. She had to cross her legs again and wait. If she hurried she would be all right. From one concrete forecourt to the next she made a rhythm, three steps and then a big step down, nearly sitting as she lowered herself level by level down the hill. She ran the last part of the pavement to her home. It was nearly dark. *Don't let her be angry because I'm late.*

"It's nearly five o'clock. Where have you been?"

9

"I was coming home."

"Don't tell me that! It doesn't take an hour from school to here. It's dark. What have you been up to? I was really worried. Give me your coat, you're frozen! Go and wash your hands and then come back to the fire. Your tea's ready. I've made you baked beans on toast. Hurry up!"

Upstairs it was dark but not frightening yet. When her Aunty Emily was here a week ago Katie had seen a bloody worm on the toilet floor. Her mother had said it was something to do with women, but she had not understood. Aunty Emily was not a real aunt, she was a friend of Mummy's. When Katie came up for her pyjamas, later, then it was frightening. But she pretended that it was not. Her sister was frightened, but she was only five. *I shall fetch my Muffin the Mule television set to play with after tea*, she decided. In the nursery she checked that all the Cellophane rolls were in the box with the plastic hand-winding, doll-sized television. She heard her name called. Clutching the box, she hurried down to the warm fire.

They felt very modern now: since Daddy died they ate their tea from their laps and they had a real television. The big shiny console stood across the corner of the breakfast room and over the nine-inch screen was screwed a large plastic magnifying-lens.

A faint light came through the open door. Once she had stayed awake and seen the red tip of her father's cigarette as he came down the corridor to their bedroom. She had whispered to him that she was still awake and he had come and sat on her bed.

She pulled back the sheet and blankets. It was icy, the lino hurt her feet. She looked down at the sleeping face of her little sister. *Please don't let her die.*

She felt compelled to bend down and kiss one of the small fat red cheeks and was surprised by the heat of the skin. She went back to bed.

When Daddy was alive she had often heard shouting and screaming downstairs, and once had gone downstairs crying. She had not been afraid but could not remember why she was crying. Her father had picked her up and then her mother had taken her and she was carried up to bed.

She had seen three or four grown-up films after they had rowed, when her mother had sometimes fetched her out of bed and they had gone out in the dark and taken the bus to the Rex Cinema, Thornton Heath. She always cried when a beautiful film-star cried, but most passionately for *Gone with the Wind* when the pony was taken to be shot — that really was unfair.

Tonight she stayed awake but nothing happened. It was a very peaceful place, now that he was dead.

2

Today was no good because there would be too
many people around on a Saturday and so the little
tree would have to be christened later when school
started again.

"You're just like your father, Katie. When there
was only one egg a week on the rations you were
crazy about them; now you never eat them. Your
father would only smoke those brands of cigarettes
that were almost unobtainable."

Her mother poured cold milk into the plate,
which was white with tiny roses painted on the rim.
The milk formed a moat around the grey circle of
cereal; Katie left its surface intact and then
embellished the centre with a thick whirl of
transparent golden syrup. Sampling each part on
its own and then slowly amalgamating all the
ingredients, she savoured the food half a spoonful
at a time.

"Come on, eat up! Do you want some bread and
marmalade?"

Katie nodded.

Her mother cut the loaf downwards but her
Granny in Wales held the loaf to her big chest and
cut the slices inward towards her body. Her
grandmother buttered the bread before she cut it,
and told Katie that she could have either butter or
jam on her bread, but not both. At home they could
always have both.

"Can I go and play with Christine, please?"

"All right, go and ask her mother but don't play in
the streets. I'm going out shopping but you're to be
back for dinner at twelve. Come here, let me put
this scarf round your neck. And try not to lose your
gloves." Her mother kissed her on the cheek.

Katie and Christine called themselves a club; the only other member was Christine's younger sister, Susan. Between them they shared the leadership in riding, swimming, tree-climbing and cycling. Since they could only afford to ride horses for half an hour a month, they were limited in practical experience in horse-womanship. They read books and talked about having ponies. Holding imaginary reins, they went trotting or cantering through their equestrian paces on foot, through the zigzag paths between the trees on the Common — their natural home, their countryside. It was country pursuits that interested them. As they rode borrowed bicycles through the suburban streets, swam in the borough pool or climbed the trees of the sparse woods they were never out of earshot of traffic. Still they knew that they really belonged in the country and that this was a time of training so that they would be ready and prepared. For the time being, however, as if by some mistake, they had to live in London.

There were always men in these woods, watching the girls, and the girls in turn would sometimes watch them. Tracking the men as they wandered furtively through sunlit clearings and in the bramble-sided worn paths, three small girls scuttled along furtively, peering over bushes, rigid behind stunted oaks and small sycamores. Katie had once seen one of these men, trousers down, yanking away at his pants. She felt sad for the men in the woods, thinking that they must be people who lived alone, without friend or family. "You must never talk to strange men!" she had been warned—Katie knew that there would be trouble if she mentioned the men. There had been a terrible fuss when the children of the Wilkinson family, who lived at the top of the hill facing the Common, had been told to take off their knickers and climb a tree. Afterwards the man had given them each sixpence — not bad for just taking off your knickers and climbing a tree. One of the Wilkinson children had told their mother and policemen had come to their house. Katie's mother had warned her never to go on the Common alone and to scream if a man came near her. She knew that she would not scream just for that.

Everything was upside down as she hung by her knees from a branch about ten feet above the ground.

"You've got to do this to pass the test, after you've climbed all the five trees in the right way!" Katie was the captain of tree-climbing. Her hat and gloves lay on the ground at the bottom of the tree between two roots.

Coming up the side of the house to the kitchen door, she suddenly had a perfect picture of the gloves. She closed her eyes. *Please, God, I will be good. Forgive me. Let them be there.* She ran back to the woods, she knew every tree, had names for most of them. She picked up the gloves and the hat and ran home.

"I thought I heard you come back five minutes ago." Her mother stood at the open door.

"I forgot something in the woods, so I had to go back."

"I suppose you nearly lost your gloves. Katie, I do wish that you'd think a little more about the things that matter. You're out all day and every day. Who would think that you had a home? You're not to go out this afternoon.

"Oh, please Mummy...."

"Stop shuffling about like that! Did you hear what I said?"

"I only want. . . ."

"Go and wash your hands. Your dinner's ready.

14

I've bought some nice sausages and there's mashed potatoes . . . I know you like that."

Katie sat in the conservatory which her father had built on to the back of the house, to cover the whole back wall. The french windows of the breakfast room and the french windows of the lounge, which were usually locked, all led into the conservatory, which joined on to the coal cupboard and the outside toilet, smelling of damp and infested with spiders. He had been good with his hands, everyone said so; Mummy had said that he was a brilliant man but always added that he had been difficult or mistreated her. Once Katie had sat there with Christine and he had come through the french windows of the lounge, wearing his dressing-gown, looking like a ghost. He was ill then, before he was taken to hospital. She remembered wishing that he was not her father. It was wicked of her, she knew that. She took out her paints, but could not think of anything to paint.

Often the conservatory made her restless. The memory of that strange morning: Mummy away, Aunty Lily (who was Granny's sister) had made them breakfast. Katie clearly remembered pasting up a newspaper of made-up news. She had done this with her sister here in the conservatory. When Mummy came back she had stood with Daddy's dressing-gown over one arm. "Your father's dead," she had said, but she need not have spoken for Katie had known without being told and felt that maybe her sister had as well. They had gone on with the newspaper.

That night Theresa had slept with Mummy and Aunty Lily had slept in the nursery with Katie. She remembered crying and crying, but trying not to make a noise. She had prayed as forcefully as possible through the silence: "*Forgive him, please, dear*

God. I know he was wicked. I was wicked. I was horrible to him. ... If he were alive now I would be kind to him, stay and read to him, not leave him alone and ill in bed. Forgive me, I am sorry. Forgive him. I loved him. I love him. I love my mother, I love my sister. I don't want Aunty Lily here now and I don't want her to hug me with her scrawny arms. Daddy, Daddy, are you really dead? I want to see you.

There remained that first doubt. *Is he really dead?* How could she know without visiting him? He had been away in the hospital for so long. He remained there even now when he was dead. *What is it like to see a dead person? What is it like to be dead?* Straight away she had known that she ought to go and see him dead but that was not allowed, it was not possible even to ask.

Afterwards Aunty Lily did not like her much, while Katie, Theresa and their mother seemed to share every feeling. They read aloud and were nearly through the New Testament before the spell dissolved. Katie returned to her Pony Club manuals. Theresa read the children's annuals. Mother read great piles of cowboy adventures from Boots' lending library — "clean honest stories", as she liked to tell them. Katie and her sister shared the comic *Girl*, delivered every Friday with *John Bull* magazine, an order for their father that had never been cancelled. Katie greatly admired the covers, which were usually idealized representations of ordinary life.

Her mother was ironing. "In Town Tonight" was on the radio. Katie looked up from the magazine, and asked if she could go to the stables the next day.

"No, Katie, I'm sorry. You must help me carry the Sevilles for marmalade back from the market, and while we're in Brixton I want to look for a new coat for you. Your school gaberdine is too short and too shabby for church. There may be enough

16

Providence cheques for Theresa to have some lace-ups as well. Look at the time! Go up and fetch the pyjamas."

Katie looked at her sister.

"Stop your teasing — off you go! When I was a young girl we slept five to a bed, all the girls in that big bed that your Granny still has."

"So where did Uncle David and Uncle Peter sleep?"

"In Granny and Grandad's room in a small bed. We none of us had nice warm pyjamas then, only vests and knickers, and they were all passed down. Oh, how I used to long to have something new, bought specially for me. You don't know how lucky you are! Often we went to bed hungry. We were the lucky ones, though; when we ate, we ate good food. Some families were always sickly. We were healthy — thank God! — although our main meal was often no more than a slice of bread and dripping."

She folded the last pillow-case and put it on the pile of ironed things, looked up and smiled at her children. Theresa yawned and continued to dress her doll, ready for bed. Katie was looking at pictures of the pygmies in the Kalahari desert, a feature of that week's *John Bull*.

Katie tried hard not to be afraid as she ran upstairs and, as quickly as possible, took a pair of pyjamas out of a zipped furry dog which lay on her bed; her sister's she found under the pillow of the other bed. Leaving the bedclothes pulled back, she scurried out of the dim room. It was a house where the upstairs landing, the stairs and the hall downstairs were all darkly full of shapes that Katie dared not look at, fearing some wicked person or persons intent on frightening her. In the warmly lit room downstairs she hung the pyjamas on the wire fire-guard. She was not really brave but always pretended to be.

Katie, in socks and liberty bodice, looked on as Theresa was helped to undress. With an affectionate slap on the little naked bottom, their mother pulled up the fleecy-lined trousers, slipped the pink top over Theresa's head and led them upstairs to their room, tucking them in with a kiss for each.

3

On Monday morning Mummy said: "It's one of those summer colds." Katie's handkerchief was slimy and sodden.

"I've rung the school. Stay indoors and keep all the doors closed."

Her mother left to go shopping, walking down the hill to Campbell's, the grocer's, and then back up the hill with a heavy basket. The grocer in Wales, where Granny lived, Mrs Cammerman, died because she ate rhubarb after the doctor had told her not to. Mrs Cammerman had said that she could not resist a little rhubarb pie and now she was dead.

There was plenty of time for Katie to go into her mother's bedroom. The big, soft, pale-green eiderdown, quilted like a huge bunch of grapes, spread over the double bed. When they were little Theresa had often climbed into bed with their parents in the morning; Katie had curled up under the eiderdown at the bottom of the bed then, alone and warm in her grey-green tent. Now she went to the kidney-shaped dressing-table and opened an embossed metal box to find inside the tiny curved leather boxes containing the most valuable and beautiful things she had ever seen. These things had to be handled with great care; she remembered nearly breaking a necklace trying to undo it. The rings were more reliable, as they slid on and off fingers but stayed on her thumbs, almost. She tried on a pair of clip-on pearl earrings. To look at the effect more closely she moved the two side mirrors and saw her own profile for the first time — it was a new person. *Not so bad*, she thought, *but I'll never be pretty*. She thought of herself as a fat-faced girl with plaits, for ever resembling the round-faced Red Indians on the films. She was saddened to think that she was not a beautiful sight.

On the shopping expedition for Katie's new coat, her mother had been sure, and the fat woman in the shop said she was right (but then she agreed with everything anyone said), that the simple fawn straight coat was the one. Katie had wished she were alone and rich; it had hurt to leave behind the red coat with the shiny buttons and to carry away the fawn one that she would hate wearing. But that afternoon Christine's sister Pamela was home from college and complimented Katie on her new coat, said that it was the perfect choice for a young girl. Katie, overwhelmed with admiration for her mother, resolved to make up for her bad feelings, knowing from past experience, however, that it would prove difficult, the exact moment might never arrive. On their mother's birthday Katie and Theresa had taken her breakfast in bed as a treat. Daddy had come down to see that everything was all right. Everything had taken such a long time. It seemed that the sausages would never cook and then, rather quickly, they looked dark brown and shrivelled. When they took the tray up, Katie knew that Daddy had told Mummy to stay in bed for an unusually long time until it did not seem like breakfast because the sun was too strong and they had been up for so long. It had not worked out quite as expected. They had never done it again.

Katie now put the rings back into their velvet slots and allowed the necklaces to curl back into their boxes, so it all looked the same as before. She went to the big dark cupboard in the corner but dared not open the low drawers since they never closed again. She stepped above them and into the mass of clothes, where she rubbed the cool satin against her cheeks, hugging and nestling against the soft fur of a squirrel coat. She had loved to see her mother sitting at the dressing-table in a petticoat, putting on her makeup, with every addition making her beauty more exquisite. The rings and the necklace followed, and then matching earrings, the long dress covered by a fur coat or a fur cape. As she kissed her little girls she smelt like a lovely flower. Daddy always grumbled, Mummy always laughed; she helped him with his tie then put on more red lipstick and the two of them would leave. Pamela was their babysitter then, sometimes with a friend. Now they were never left in the night because Mummy always stayed at home.

Behind the clothes on the floor of the cupboard stood a slightly broken cardboard box containing photographs. Its lid was decorated with pink, mauve and red flowers, like giant sweet-peas, against a black background. Lifting it revealed two black ribbons provided to support the open lid. The photographs started to slip out. Daddy as a soldier, Mummy as a girl guide, Mummy as a nurse, Theresa as a baby, Katie as a baby, some aunts, some uncles, some cousins, some unknown people. Right at the bottom there were two big shiny photographs, their edges bent to fit into the box. Taken at night, the first picture showed figures that shone out as they advanced towards the camera. Daddy in an evening suit with a lady in a long shiny dress, a fur coat resting over the narrow straps on her otherwise bare shoulders, and she was smiling, and wearing lipstick and had hair that was curly and blonde. The second showed Daddy in military uniform, standing on the grass, and there she was again: blonde, in a nearly tight suit, a dark hat pulled sideways over her head, she stood next to him, a cigarette in hand. Katie always looked hard at the lady's face in these photographs, trying to know her. Who could tell if she were good or not? Certainly she was beautiful. It was always difficult to make all the pictures stay in the box but once they were in it was easy to hide them back in the dark again.

In the furthest corner, right at the back of the cupboard, a black metal urn could be found, flowers painted on it, and in curly writing under RIP were all of Katie's Christian names — Katerina, Carlotta and Maria — she hated it when they read out your full names at the beginning of term and wished she were called Susan or Janet. Why did she have to have all these funny names? On the top of the lid was a little knob but it was impossible to look inside because it was fixed down. The whole thing was unnaturally lightweight.

Once downstairs, Katie could only pretend to read until her mother's return.

Because she had a cold her mother had bought her one of her favourite cakes, an iced bun. Iced buns were difficult to eat, needing nice judgement not to end up with mouthfuls of dry crumby bun and no icing, but instead to finish with a slice of crumb and a thick crust of icing.

While her mother did the washing, Katie wandered about the house. The dining-room was brown, walls in shiny paper to look like wood panels, six chairs showing high ornate backs above a polished walnut table-top while two stood sternly on guard beside the cupboard. The fire surround, with two mantel shelves, was dark wood; the square carpet was a reddish-brown patterned Indian; the seating around the jutting-out window had cushions brown-ridged against a blue-grey background. Until recently, up until her father's death, the mantelpieces and the cupboard top had been laden with silver cups. They were all gone now because they were dust traps — more work for Mummy. Katie sat on the window seat, pulled the long red velvet curtain around her and, pushing the edge of the net curtain aside, saw the empty road with two smaller houses on the other side that were different from the others in the street. The net curtain had been stretched taut between two brass rods fixed at the top and bottom of the window. Reaching up, she could knock the wooden acorn that swung on a cord from the dark green blind ratcheted at exactly the same level as all the others, one in each window.

The piano was still in the lounge. Katie had often lain underneath the piano when her father had played "The War March of the Priests" by Mendelssohn, the vibration of the music roaring in her ears and through her whole body. When he played melodies by Chopin she could nearly cry.

No one played the piano properly any more. Its top was kept closed and Mummy had covered it with her black fringed Spanish shawl and placed on it a framed photograph of herself as a nurse. Still, despite the great loss of music, the lounge remained a voluptuous place. You could sit on the arms of the feathered-cushioned chairs and then slide backwards and almost disappear, down and down into the soft deepness. Over the grey carpet were fur rugs; the furniture was curved and friendly art-nouveau ebony. The walls had been one of Daddy's summer surprises. On their return from their holidays in Wales — in the summer Daddy always had a surprise for them — the walls were papered in silver. They had come back before he had finished putting up all the borders and corner pieces that he had bought in Belgium and Mummy said, "Enough is enough .... They border everything in Belgium."

There were fireplaces in every room, even in the hall. If Katie or her sister was ill there would be a fire in the nursery. On Sundays a fire was lit in the lounge. The only time that all the downstairs fires were lit was on Christmas Day, the most beautiful morning of the year. With all the fires sparkling, little bowls of sweets and nuts set out, huge bowls of holly, decorations and presents, everything was jolly until during the afternoon when it became a bit stuffy and they began to see what Mummy meant when she said it would be no fun to have more than one Christmas a year.

While Mummy went out again, to collect Theresa from school, Katie put the cups and saucers out ready for tea. She could lay the table, do the ironing and clean as well as her mother could — she had heard her mother tell people that. Now that she tried to wash her slimy handkerchiefs she realized she was no good at washing clothes.

It was still light after school, even at bedtime. Christine called to see her while they were having tea. She had brought along the school milk and a straw for Katie, which was allowed when someone was ill, according to the rules, although it was really no more than an excuse to go and visit them at home. The bottle had a layer of cream at the top; school milk tasted different from home milk and had a strong smell. It reminded Katie of school which reeked of milk, wooden floors and pee. Most people's houses had special smells; Mrs Barnes's across the road smelt of Bovril and reminded Katie of silence. Only their own house had no smell. It just seemed warm when you came in — though maybe to other people it did have a particular smell.

When Katie asked to go out with her friend, Mummy said, "All right then, only a short walk. I suppose it might do you good. Wrap up warm!"

"Come on, Katie, come to my house! I *must* take my uniform off."

At the back of the woods was a stream full of leaves and mud where the sun never reached. The stream passed beneath the path that joined the Common to the park. The water was impeded by a rusty iron grid, piled high with leaves, that protected the entrance to the pipe culvert passing under the path. This year the girls could, after summoning up their courage, jump across the stream channel, from one brick wall to the other. The leap reached the cement parapet capping the brick wall and was followed by a further step on to clear ground before reaching a broken wooden fence. Katie and Christine, holding hands, still excited by their daring, walked cautiously along the narrow ledge, taking care not to slip down into the channel. Shrubs and trees tumbled over the fence. Pushing a piece of wood sideways, they climbed over the lower horizontal timber of the fence. The paths of the garden were still recognizable where they curled around abandoned flower-beds and clumps of shrubs. The heady smell of syringa stopped them at a spot spiky with flowers, where the dead eyes of a fallen statue stared absently through a clump of wide-open daisies. It was the edge of a lawn, now grown meadow-high and floral. Branches of a tree twirled about above them and they stroked the lumpy plaited trunk that grew sideways instead of straight up. They knew it was a mulberry tree, unique and secret to them.

4

She was, for a change, early coming back from school; she had a note to take to her mother. The sun was still shining as she walked past the garages. The little sycamore had six leaves that looked too big for it, as though it had dressed up in grown-up's clothes. No one was in the house. Katie found her mother on the raised bank that ran along the back of the garden, where two apple trees grew. Theresa was crouching over some bare ground at the left-hand side of the garden beyond the shed, the spare coal-bunker and the flagpole near the top of the steps from the conservatory, where Katie now stood surveying the small and elaborate garden which her father had planned before she was born. Her mother pulled the smaller girl up by a hand and led the way into the house.

The Wilkinsons lived in half a house that had doors which were difficult to open because the handles were very high. Their home was light, it was nearly untidy and a happy place. The three girls left the two women sitting in the front room talking. Katie and Theresa urged Linda, who was the same age as Katie (but went to a different school), to let them play with the dressing-up box. The best thing was a dress that had belonged to Aunty Stella's grandmother, who must have been very small, as the dress was only just too big for them. They paraded back into the front room. Uncle James, who was an artist, arrived home at that moment. He was famous for his drawings for Guinness and Bovril advertisements.

Mummy said that it was extravagant to live like Aunty Stella, who did not bake her own cakes or make jam or do anything like that. Now Mummy was telling Aunty Stella, in a lowered voice, that Katie was not doing very well at school.

"She's not like Theresa. She has to learn the hard way, so it might do her good to stay down for a year." Her voice picked up and she was smiling at the company as though pleased with everyone. "Aunty Stella asks if you'd like some silkworms, Katie?"

"Oh, yes, please. Where will I keep them, Mummy?"

"They can stay in the outside coal-house, next to the breakfast room, until the coal comes in the autumn. You'll have to look after them yourself. Don't expect me to help you."

"What do they need to eat?"

Aunty Stella said: "I have a friend with a pet shop. You know the one in the arcade opposite the swimming-baths. She'll sell you mulberry leaves. That's all they need — plus a few drops of water."

Turning away from Katie towards her mother, Aunty Stella continued: "I wonder if you know her, Mary? Ann Foster — she belongs to our Church. She has an Indian spirit-guide and she breeds Irish setters. They're supposed to be very good — they win prizes."

"You know that Mary doesn't want anything to do with your spiritualism, Stella, nor is she interested in dogs, as far as I know," said Uncle James, with a smile.

"I like dogs. It's not that I'm wholly against it — your beliefs, you understand — but it seems to me to go against the teaching of Christ. I believe that we should only need Him and His salvation. I think it may not be right to try and contact the dead. We should have faith and not seek to know more than that."

"We've had these arguments so many times,

Mary dear. James doesn't agree with me either. But you should try to come to one of our meetings, you really should. You'll be amazed."

"Yes, I would like to come. I'd have to find a minder for the girls, though."

Was it wrong, then, Katie wondered, to ask God to help Daddy? But what she said aloud was: "I know where there's a mulberry tree."

Her mother looked rather surprised at this piece of information.

"You must go and see Ann then. She'll pay you for the leaves, I should think, since there's a silkworm craze at the moment, " said Aunty Stella.

5

Behind a plate-glass window, on a bed of yellow fake straw, puppies, white and black, were curled up or tumbling about. Their attention was only held for a few seconds as Katie tapped the window. The door opened with a tinkling bell. She had brought the leaves. Yes, her satchel was full of them, and her right hand was stiff from gripping another neat pile upon which her fingers had made dark green spots. Pushing aside a curtain behind the counter at the back of the shop, part of a woman emerged, but her head remained behind the curtain for a while. The woman stepped backwards another pace before turning and looking beyond, then down, at Katie, neither smiling nor changing her expression as she gazed at the child.

"I've brought you these mulberry leaves because Mrs Wilkinson said that you wanted some," Katie explained.

The woman stood quietly looking at her, then moved her lips slightly back in about a quarter of a smile. Katie's small stiff hand, full of leaves, was held out in front of her.

"Put them on the counter."

Katie emptied the satchel. Released, the leaves moved, and the pile expanded, grew to look quite big by the time the last limp leaf was taken from the bottom of the bag.

The woman went behind the curtain again and came back with a brown carrier bag. The leaves more than half-filled it. She put the bag on the floor behind the counter.

"Thank you. So you know Stella Wilkinson, do you? Would you like some tea? I've just made some."

The bell tinkled as two men walked in to the shop and stood waiting, their faces lit by the rippling green light from the aquarium on the wall.

The woman took no immediate notice of them but pulled the side of the curtain back. "Go on in! I'll come in a minute."

Katie walked past the woman, under her arm, through to the back of the shop as the woman turned to see to the men.

The room was rather small, filled, it seemed, with furniture and smells. The walls were painted a pretty blue above, and below everything was dark-coloured. She stood just inside, behind the curtain, nearly touching a table covered in newspapers, some in piles. There were also cups and plates, some dirty, and one blue and white striped mug that was clean and stood beside a steaming brown teapot, all spread out on a sheet of newspaper. Dark shapes stirred. Two very big, black and brown dogs lifted themselves off a small sofa. Further in, beyond the table against the far wall was a chair that matched the sofa, wooden-slatted with balding brown velvet; this was taken up by another similar dog. On the floor on a rug in the middle of the lino a fourth dog stirred, walked slowly over, sniffed her crotch, put its head up, looked her in the face and took another sniff. She put a hand out to stroke it, just feeling the silky fur on its skull as it moved backwards, turned a few times and sat on a newspaper on the floor between a gas stove and the sink in the right-hand corner of the room. She stepped into the middle of the room and on to the rug, surprised to see that it was woven from old stockings many shades of brown.

The woman came in behind her. "Get down, Jason!" The dog slipped easily off the chair and stood shaking itself in front of Katie. "Do, please, sit down!"

Katie sat on the edge of the warm, flattened cushion, her arms resting lightly on the wooden chair arms. Holding the handle of a mug of tea, she balanced it on one of the arms. The tea was nearly too hot to drink, but made with sterilized milk: she loved that. Her Aunty Fran — she was a real aunt — used it. At home they always used gold-top milk, because it was better.

Two dogs came and sniffed her, their noses touched her face.

"Go away, both of you! Don't worry about them, they won't hurt you. Have you seen Irish setters before?"

"No, only red setters. I like these more."

The woman sat, one leg crossed over the other, on a hard chair at the table. She smiled at Katie's words. She looked up at a painting hanging on the wall above the table. "That's a picture of Chief Cochee. He's my spirit guide. I had never painted a picture before in my life but I was guided by him to paint.... Stella never painted either, but she paints lovely pictures, now. It's not really her who paints them — it's the spirits, of course."

The woman rubbed a wandering dog's back, lifting its face up and giving it a big kiss on the nose.

Katie, too, stroked a dog that stood nearby.

"I ought to go home now," she said, not wanting to ask for any money. Now that did not matter much because it was nice here. She put the mug on the table, where there was only just room for it. As Katie was walking out of the shop, Ann came up beside her and, opening the door, she gave her a half-crown.

Running and walking back towards home, her light satchel swinging against her back, Katie felt like shouting with joy. All the way she fingered the coin in her dress pocket.

6

The numbers made Katie's head hurt, trying to sort out additions, subtractions, multiplications and divisions from one group of figures to another, all jumbled up on the blackboard. Since it was hopeless, she bent an arm over her desk to hide her books and her idiocy and waited, stranded in a horrible maze, for the teacher's understandable exasperation and anger to find her out.

Afternoon classes ended with a lovely period when they were all read a story. Then Katie stood with the others to say grace, with her eyes tightly closed: "Please, God, let me feel your hand in mine: give me a sign — just a small sign, of your closeness." She opened her eyes to the banging of desk lids. She lifted the top of her desk to take out her cardigan; unhooked her satchel from the back of the chair and put her box of pencils in it; left the smell of the school for the fresh air and light of the streets.

On this particular Monday there were two of them. They walked behind her and she dared not look back, but she could hear them laughing. Her dress was not caught up, so she decided that her walk felt funny.

Near the garages they called her. "Girlie! Come here, girlie! We want to ask you some questions."

She turned and the two big boys rushed at her and pushed her backwards between two of the garages. As she glimpsed the sycamore she thought: *Help me!*

"We know that you steal school pencils. You're a thief. The police will come to your house."

There was no answer to this. Maybe she had — things seemed to happen without her knowing. She could not remember ever taking school pencils but they had masses of pencils at home. One of the boys pinned her by her shoulders to the concrete side wall, while the other grabbed her satchel, took out the pencil box and hit her on the head with it. She started to cry.

"Girls always cry. You're a stupid girl." They were pinching her all over as she sobbed and wriggled. "If you tell anyone you'll be in trouble." Then they ran away, dropping her things.

She did not have a handkerchief, her nose was dripping, but there were no more tears. She picked up the satchel and put the box back in it, then picked up her cardigan; she wanted to rub her face and blow her nose on it but was too afraid to do it, so she just took the drip away with a bit of the woolly and rubbed the patch between her knuckles to make the liquid go away.

Once she had reached home she wanted to go straight upstairs. Her mother was near the kitchen door as she came in.

"Come here, Katie! You've been crying — what's the matter?"

"Nothing's the matter."

"Has something happened at school? Tell me and I promise I won't be angry."

Mummy was so good and kind and right that she must not know about all these horrible things — the dark and wicked part of Katie's life.

"I've got a tummy-ache." (God forgive her for lying.) "Let Mummy kiss you better." Katie clung to her mother. "Are you sure that nothing else is wrong?"

"I've just got a tummy-ache," said Katie, safe and very well indeed, now. *I'm all right now. When I'm big I'll capture little children and torture them. Let the night be very long....*

34

Once in bed, Katie realized that she was being punished for being so horrible to her father. She wondered if Daddy knew the Red Indians. There seemed to be a lot of Indians in heaven; maybe that was why she had felt as though she might be part of their brotherhood when she had seen them on the films. "Forgive me, Daddy," she whispered. "I want to be good, not just for me but for you too — but things seem to be getting worse. . . . Mummy's coming up to bed so it must be very late. I wish she'd come to get me out of bed and we'd go to see a film now."

As her mother handed her a bowl of porridge she said, "You were screaming in the night, Katie. I'm coming to see your teacher after school this afternoon," she added, with undue emphasis.

"Oh, please don't."

"How's your tummy this morning?"

"It's still there.... but not very much." She could not, even now, let the deceit stop.

"Have you forgotten Miss Lee asked to see me? Don't go — wait for me, do you hear, after school is over!" "Yes, Mummy."

"Off you go now, or you'll be late!"

"Yes, Mummy."

As the day slipped by, Katie hardly noticed the lessons, even PT, when it was her turn to be monitor and to put the hoops, bean-bags and coloured bands back into the games cupboard and then be late for the next lesson because the cupboard had to be locked and the key taken to the secretary. The whole day was just a dreadful wait for her mother coming to the school. Sometimes, as the thoughts whirled round her head, Katie felt that it would be a relief if her mother knew all about her: then it would be over. Nothing could be worse;

she could start again, make a fresh, unsullied beginning and be good and honest for the rest of her life.

It turned out not to be awful. While the two women talked, Katie stood by. She heard her mother say, "I can't understand it. Her sister's getting on so well," and it did not really seem to be her they were discussing but some grown-up stuff about children and school.

She walked the normal way home with her mother. Her mother knew nothing of the secrets of the overgrown pathway, although they passed it now, nor did she know the secrets of around the garages.

"Katie, listen to me. You really must try harder. You're not a naughty girl, but I'm disappointed in you, and I know that your father would be too if he were here."

"Yes, Mummy." She meant it, although not exactly then, as she was saying the words, because the main things seemed to exist in the dark and did not have words. Children who had nice names and lived in small houses with ordinary mothers and fathers lived in a world open with words. Mummy was like that. She, Katie, was like Daddy: he was different. No, that was not quite right because he had been good. He would go to heaven. Certainly Katie would help him.

"What would you like for your tea? Poached egg on toast or baked beans? I've bought you a bun for afterwards. I was thinking....I think I can afford to buy you a pair of jeans like the Barclays have. Theresa can have some as well."

"I don't need any pocket money any more because I sell the leaves to the woman in the pet shop." It must be like that to live in the country: you grew things and ate and sold things and it was simple and you had a lot of animals.

Katie took out the cups and saucers to lay the table for tea. When she grew up, she would have mugs and live in the country and let dogs sit on chairs. She and her sister moved their chairs around and ate from the plates on their laps while they watched Muffin the Mule on television.

7

Katie watched as her mother and sister, hand in hand, walked down the hill to the shops. She crossed the road on to the Common, over an unmade strip of road where last year a gang of red-faced men had shouted and laughed at them while digging a huge trench right up the hill, for the drains. Afterwards she heard that two of them had been killed when earth fell on top of them. In their own garden, below about a foot deep, the soil was thick, sticky, yellow clay. It was strange to think that just earth, falling on you, could kill you. Every time as she passed the filled-in trench she wondered if it had been any of the jolly faces that had been buried.

Here at the top of the Common, where you could see houses and churches below and the great cooling towers of Croydon beyond, the ground was springy and the grass tufted and wiry. Further down, where the ground was flatter, the grass had wider, greener blades and resembled the grass in the garden. She crossed over a road and walked past the top paddling-pool that was concrete and round with a path and a parapet, just like the one at the bottom of the Common opposite the church. Mothers shouted, sitting on the wall at the edge, while children splashed and screamed in the water at the centre.

She continued walking up the dappled middle path through the woods, turning off before coming to the road that curled round the summit to join it. Four tall pines fanned above the small clearing through which she passed to reach the worn grey-yellow tracks to the dried stream bed, down and up, then she pulled herself straight on the wooden fence. The fence moved and she pushed it aside and climbed through into the garden. Standing beside the mulberry tree, she gazed at the broken house with canopy of twisted metal waving above a low veranda, where rusty steps joined gnarled wrought-iron railings. She wondered if it would be very difficult to mend the house and decided that it would not and that she would like to make it look all new and nice again. She pulled herself up into the tree and began picking the leaves, carefully, one at a time. Quite unaware of her presence, a man had entered the garden and was walking across the lawn towards the tree. He stopped right underneath it and lit a cigarette, turned, watched the thrown match land on the grass, then walked on right below her and on out of the garden. Motionless, she waited but he did not return. This week she had brought a carrier bag for the leaves which was now nearly full and dangled by the string handles from her mouth as she climbed down. On the ground by the tree had been dropped a bright red and white packet which, when she picked it up, she found nearly full of cigarettes, so she put it on top of the mulberry leaves in the bag.

The pet shop was so crowded that she waited outside by the door, looking in through the window, watching the puppies. This week there were three: last week there had been eight. She knew that the dogs cost ten shillings and the bitches seven shillings and sixpence. She had wanted the tiniest bitch and it was still there, but Mummy said that she could not have it because she would not look after it. That was not true. She had been sad and angry and had been sent to bed early for making a fuss. If she had a dog she would love to have it sleep on her bed, which Mummy would never allow — but still she wanted a dog, even if it had to sleep downstairs. Most of the people had left the shop and as two left, one of them carrying a goldfish in a jam jar, Katie went through the open door.

The woman was straightening some papers on the counter. "Hello — how kind you are," she said, taking the bag and again putting it on the floor behind the counter. "I haven't had a minute's peace all this morning. It's really still too early but I'm going to close for lunch. There are more important things in life than work, don't you agree?"

Katie started to think about the question but did not get very far.

"Would you like to eat here? You'll have to wait while I cook."

"Yes," replied Katie and, because she thought she ought to say no, she added, "but...."

"Had you better tell your mother? Do you have a phone?"

"Yes."

"Well, you decide. There's enough food here. Help yourself to the phone." She pointed to the telephone at the edge of the counter. "Maybe your mother's expecting you home."

Katie dialled their number.

"Katie, are you all right? Where are you speaking from?"

"I'm at the pet shop. Please, can I have dinner here?"

"Has she asked you to stay and eat?"

"Yes."

"Well, if you're sure, that's very kind of her. Be a good girl and remember to say please and thank you — we'll see you this afternoon. Aunty Emily is coming to tea."

Katie put the receiver down and walked cautiously into the room behind the curtain.

Everything was the same as the first time, except for a nutty smell coming from a saucepan on the gas stove.

She sat down at the table. The woman was nowhere to be seen. One by one the dogs came over and nuzzled her. She stroked them but none stayed for long. The table was still covered in newspapers, mugs and teaspoons which she felt that she should clear, but maybe that would be interfering. She sat and waited. The woman came in from the door at the back of the room. Evidently she had heard enough of the telephone conversation to understand that Katie would stay because she went straight to the stove, lifted the lid off the saucepan, waved the steam away to look inside and then put the lid back. She pushed a dog off a chair, slumped into it, crossed her legs and took a pack of cigarettes out of her trouser pocket. She lit a cigarette with a match and settled down to inhale the smoke.

Katie, remembering with a slight start the red and white packet she had found, stood up and quietly crept out to the shop counter where she took the cigarettes from on top of the leaves. She walked back and stood in the centre of the room, holding the packet out in front of her towards the sprawled woman, who sat up, smiled, and accepted it.

"What's this? Do you smoke?"

Was it good or bad, Katie wondered, that she had said that?

"I don't know your name?" asked the woman.

"Katie. . . Katerina, really."

"Well, mine is Ann."

It would be difficult to call a grown-up by a single name, thought Katie. It would be like being a grown-up — just a proper name.

"Can I lay the table or do anything. . . Ann?"

41

"Thanks, you just sit there."

Ann presented her with a bowl of rice, but not as a pudding. There seemed to be some cabbage in it, on top of which were slices of bananas and some peanuts. On the cupboard Ann found a small bottle of dark brown liquid. "Do you want some soya sauce?"

"I don't know. I never tried it."

"Here, sniff the bottle. I'll leave it on the table."

Spooning it up, a little at a time, Katie thought that the tastes were nice and miraculously all these funny things went well together. Her sister Theresa would never eat it: she did not even like ordinary food.

"It's lovely, this food. I never ate anything like it before — what's it called?"

"I don't know. I just cook whatever I have at the moment. Leave the plate there on the table, and let's have a cup of tea."

She put the kettle on. "Well, Katie, I owe you a lot of money now, for the leaves and the cigarettes. By the way, does your mother smoke? Where did the cigarettes come from?"

"No, I found them. My father used to smoke — nearly all the time — but now he's dead."

"When did he die?"

"In the winter when I was nine and I'll be ten in September. On September the third."

"It wasn't very long ago that he died then, was it?"

"I was wondering. . . Ann. . . do you really know some dead Indians? I mean, that is, to speak to?"

"I have my spirit guide. He is always somewhere nearby. He watches over me. But I can't just chat to him like I can to you. There are some people who are what we call psychic. We call them mediums. They are very sensitive and when they stay very

42

quiet and calm they can sometimes hear and see the spirits that are around us." She handed Katie a mug of tea. "Stella and I go to a church, which is in a house in Brixton. A lot of people go there and often there are messages for them from the spirit world."

"Can you hear God?"

"No. Only the people who have passed on can, but they are doing God's work by helping us here on earth."

"Can we help the spirits?"

"I never thought of that, but I'm sure we can. It must please them to comfort their loved ones left on earth."

"My mother thinks that Aunty Stella's wrong. She says that she's going to go to your church, but that she doesn't need any more than believing in God and Jesus and the Bible."

"But we believe in those as well. . . . Let's see what she thinks once she has been, shall we?"

"Can I come too?"

"I don't see why not — except that we never do have any children there. Also I'm pretty sure that your mother won't want you to come."

"It's rather important. . . . I don't really know how to explain. I can't tell you exactly. . . . But if you could help me I can come here, I can walk your dogs, clean the shop and maybe I can do lots of jobs for you. Please take me to Brixton."

"I'd have to ask. . . . Why don't you ask your mother?"

Katie's heart sank. She knew her mother would not take her. She could not even start to ask her. There would be questions and problems — even fibs (lies was too terrible a word); this was no good. If Ann would not help her, she had no hope. She looked up at the Indian in the painting: his eyes stared down at her. *Give me strength*, came to her

43

mind. She wondered if she should ask God for forgiveness for nearly praying to the Indian but she did not feel bad and the eyes still held her gaze. She wished at him to help her. Maybe she was a medium, that is, providing she was not bad, maybe. Sometimes you could wish miracles. It would be like that to be grown up and choose what you wanted to do.

The dog called Jason was pulling hard against its collar. Before they were halfway up the Common he had his tongue out, panting. As they reached the middle, Katie dropped the lead. The dog sprang away and with bounding strides was nearly at the top of the hill, too far away to hear her screaming and shouting his name. She was panting, her voice had grown shaky and she felt that she was going to fall down and cry and just lie there for ever more until she died. Jason circled about and was now bounding down the hill, passing her, not noticing his name. She ran down the hill, fast, but not fast enough to catch up. Then Jason just stopped and stood with perfect obedience. *O God, oh, thank you. Let him stay there, let him stand still.* She approached the dog, who stood a picture of tranquillity and beauty. When she grabbed the lead he sat down and Katie flung her arms around his neck. It was not his fault; Katie had noticed that dogs never obey children — only adults, and not even all adults. When she had a dog of her own it would love and obey her, like Lassie or Rin Tin Tin or the other dogs of the film world.

Her mother agreed that Jason was a beautiful dog and gave Katie a biscuit to give him.

Her sister stroked his head. "Can we keep it here, Katie?"

"No, of course not, it's not ours. I've got to take it

back now. We must ask Mummy if we can have a dog, a puppy — you ask her, because I've asked lots of times. If we had a puppy it could join our club."

"Yes! Could it sleep with me in my bed?"

"No, it would have to learn to sleep in the kitchen. I've got to go now. See you later and don't forget to ask — right?"

8

Since there were now only two weeks until they went away on holiday, however difficult or scary, she needed to discover the house that was a church. Trembling a little, she looked through some of the piles of paper that sat on the table and in the upturned orange-box that acted as a cupboard next to the stove. Ann had one day said that she would be happy to use nothing but orange-boxes for furniture. Katie tried the idea out on her mother, who had not been completely against it, because it would save polishing and you could just throw them away when they broke. Obviously, though, she had not really taken the idea seriously.

Katie looked towards the ever-watching eyes of the Indian. *Help me!* This time it worked. Out fell a postcard. Not a picture postcard but one with an address underlined in black, printed along the top: 14 Pencil Lane, Brixton Hill, SW18. That surely must be the place. The handwritten message below read: "Meeting at 3pm, followed by tea." She was unable to read the date of the postmark, but now she had the address.

She felt an enormous sense of achievement and relief that Ann's abrupt return through the curtain did not make her start as she often did when she had done nothing. She stood with the card still in her hand, not caring. Ann took no notice, walking straight past and out into the yard where the lavatory was.

"See to them if anyone comes into the shop," she called. "I won't be long. I think you do better than me for the business anyway!"

Probably not true, Katie thought as she stood behind the counter. She loved serving in the shop. She could do nearly everything, like weighing the biscuits and the grains. She knew all the prices; she could do the money; fish out the fish and she knew to put them in the same water from the tank. They kept a shelf of jam jars under the counter; there were cardboard boxes for hamsters and budgies, just for taking them home, but they also sold wooden boxes and cages. Only the budgies made her nervous. She hated the feel of their tiny bodies under such soft quilly coats. In her dreams there was a world filled with feathers and Indians. Time and again she recoiled from these plumed dreams.

Katie looked into the money drawer, wondering if she should go and ask for some change before the post office closed at half-past five. Ann stayed open until six o'clock for the people coming home from work. Katie could imagine that without this extra time hundreds of pets would go hungry, if not die. They sold a lot of pieces off a block of bright red, rather crumbly meat called Doggy Special. Katie did not dare to ask if this had horsemeat in it. Life was difficult enough trying to do the right things without looking for more problems; such an attitude was wrong and uncourageous, she knew. Pecking at a few crumbs of the pink meat, she decided that it did not taste too bad. She had tried, at one time or another, nearly all the pet foods, kept loose in bins in front of the counter. She had imagined that they might make her able to run faster.

9

Someone would surely see her and she would be found out, she thought, as she stood on the kerb, wondering why the b—— bus did not come. Because she had heard her father say "bloody" she had once repeated it and Mummy smacked her and told her never to say it again. Being too frightened to climb the stairs, she stayed downstairs, going right to the front of the bus and looking out like the driver. This trip was no fun, she decided, spoilt by her fear that the conductor would know that she was supposed to be at school. However, he took the fare without comment and before they reached Brixton Hill she was beginning to enjoy the ride.

She got off at a stop requested by a fat woman with a small suitcase. She would not ask, being sure that she would find it if she walked all the way down the hill and looked at every street. She must be careful not to attract suspicion. The prison was somewhere near here, though she could not be sure whether she was passing it or not, as there were so many horrible-looking buildings that had always frightened her when seeing them from the bus. There were blocks of dwellings covered in brown tiles from which probably emerged the children who had their lessons separately and still wet their knickers and would go on to special horrible schools.

Finally she had reached the right road. She rubbed her forehead, which had water on it — not sweat like horses, but perspiration. Her armpits tingled. She made her way down the road, walking rather quickly, passing coloured people sitting on a wall. Brixton was famous for having lots of coloured people. It was true what Mummy had said, that they loved bright clothes and did not seem to mind wearing colours that clashed. She was a bit frightened of them and hurried along as though she were on some important business, looking at the numbers every now and then.

She need not have bothered. Over the front gate to number fourteen was an arch proclaiming: DEATH IS NOT THE END AND WE CAN PROVE IT. Otherwise it was like the rest of the terrace, red brick, with a square window jutting out that took up nearly the whole of the front garden but left enough room for two dustbins standing in one corner. The door was set back in a square porch; above it was coloured glass with the number fourteen written in it. A prominent black knocker curved out from high above the central wood panel, while at the side of the door, lower down, she found a round plastic bell. She pushed and could hear a loud buzz. It seemed a long wait before the door opened.

In the dim hallway stood a man. "Yes?"

"I. . . . Please, I would like to see the medium."

"I though it must be the bob-a-job. We've had three of them here already today. Who do you want to see, exactly?"

"The medium. . . . Ann, that is Miss Foster, said that maybe I could see her. . . or. . . ." She wanted more than anything to go away. An ancient smell emerged from the house, through the half-open front door, that included mothballs.

"Miss Foster said that, did she? Well, just wait a minute. Look, perhaps you'd better come inside." He stepped back and fully opened the door to allow her through, then closed it. Coloured blobs of light shone on the tiles of the floor. "Come on in here!" He opened a door off the passageway into a room well supplied with comfortable chairs and a few low

49

tables. There was also a notice-board and several paintings hung on the walls.

Katie sank down right into the back of the low chair, her knees sticking up in the air, facing a picture of clouds with the sun shining it's rays upwards, a bird floating up in the rays, and all a bit misty. The man returned shortly with an old woman. She was heavy, hard-bodied, with grey hair held in tight discipline with a hairnet. She smiled at Katie, and her face seemed kind with the eyes of a very good person.

"My name is Ursula. May I ask yours?"

"Katie — that's short for Katerina."

"Where do you live, Katie?"

"In Streatham, near the Common."

"Now tell me what we can do for you. You look quite hot. Would you like some lemonade, perhaps?"

"No, thank you," replied Katie, although it was not really true but it seemed a funny day already. "Are you a medium, Ursula?" she asked, pronouncing the name with a *sh* sound — she ought to have practised it in her head first.

"Do you know what it means to be a medium, Katie?"

"Yes. . . the spirits trust you."

"I ought to tell you that I am a medium. Can you tell me why you want to see a medium? Is it to contact someone who has passed on?"

At last she was getting somewhere, Katie realized, thankful that she had not gone away, that she had been brave. "My father died and I want to talk to him."

"You must understand that even mediums cannot just talk to the spirits of those who have passed on. Just sometimes we're privileged to be able to pass back a message to those who remain here on earth. What is it you have to tell your father that's so important?"

"It's difficult to say exactly. I really ought to speak to him. I'm sorry now that I didn't like him sometimes. I'm very sorry that I was unkind to him when he was ill. I want to know about him now. . . . No, not now, really, but about him then, when he was alive. But I do want him to be good. I know that he wanted to be good — he was good really — God will forgive him." There seemed to be light surrounding Katie and as it gradually faded away she saw the woman looking at her. There were tears streaming down Katie's face.

"Here, have this handkerchief. I'll fetch you some lemonade."

What was going on Katie did not know, nor did it seem to matter much at the moment. She had told the truth. She could only wait. She blew her nose and sipped the lemonade, which was the same sort that they had at home.

"Now listen, Katie, I've just phoned Ann Foster. You know that she's your friend, don't you?"

"Yes, I do."

"She has just told me a little bit about you, she said what a good girl you are and how much you help her. I think she knows a friend of your mother's, Stella Wilkinson. That's right, isn't it? We won't tell your mother anything about your visit — that is, unless you want us to."

"Oh, please. Don't tell her. Please don't!"

"No, I promise. Now listen to me carefully: it's quite natural that you should be very sad because your father's dead. Everyone feels very sad and it's strange when someone they've loved dies, that is to say. . . goes away from them. But they're there in the next world, you know. You can be quite sure that your father knew that you loved him. Before he had to leave you, he was an old man and he was sick, so it was quite understandable that you didn't like to see him too much. He understood that. It wasn't wrong of you — it was quite normal in the circumstances. He didn't have to forgive you, because he loved you. He loved both his little girls and he loved your mother. You're the eldest child, so you'll have to help your mother. One day you will grow up to be a beautiful woman like her, and your father will be proud of you."

It all sounded true. Why, Katie wondered, had she not thought of this herself? "Will you ask him for me?"

"I will try and contact him, if you like. Are you feeling all right, Katie?"

"Yes, I want to hear him once."

"I am very sorry, really, I am. But we don't allow children to our meetings. You can come here again though, one afternoon, and then we can talk. Aren't you supposed to be at school this afternoon?"

"Yes."

"Well, let's not mind about that for the moment. How did you come here?"

"On the fifty-nine bus."

"I'll ask Henry to take you to the bus stop. You come back again on Saturday afternoon, if that's possible. I would like very much to see you again. And don't worry about your father. Theirs is a much better world, more beautiful than we can imagine. Just think of that. You should be happy for him and not make him sad for you. I think you'd better go home now, before your mother wonders what's happened to you."

She kissed Katie on the forehead. It felt as if God was near.

"Henry. Please would you take this young lady to

the fifty-nine bus stop — the one travelling south."

Henry was standing by the open front door.

"Goodbye, my dear," she called to Katie.

"Goodbye!" replied Katie.

Henry held her hand as they walked together along the pavement and she did not seem to mind.

Oh, dear, thought Katie at the bus stop, *I forgot to say thank you.*

10

They had a suitcase between them, together with another small one, which she had promised to keep by her, since it had the money for her aunt in it. She had some coins — two shillings — in a handkerchief in her pocket, to spend when the coach stopped at Crawley, half-way to Brighton. The coach was late. They waited at the bottom of the Common, the only people at the stop. Katie glanced up at the Common for a last look at the houses that ran up the side to where the end of their road could be seen. Brighton was not so far away, she thought, doubtfully. When they went to Wales by coach she was always sick, while going to Brighton she just felt ill but was not actually sick. Travelling by train was much nicer but cost a lot more money. They could see their coach coming now.

"Remember to be good girls and help Aunty Betty. Don't forget to give her the money in the envelope in the small case. Have a lovely time darlings! Aunty will meet you at the other end. If she's not there, just wait for her, do you understand?"

Yes, they understood, they assured their mother, kissing her before climbing into the coach, which was only half full. The driver put their suitcase on the rack. Theresa sat next to the window. By agreement, they would change places half-way. They waved until they could no longer see their mother.

The coach, with its horrible groaning engine and that special smell which alone was enough to make Katie feel sick, passed through the dusty grey streets of South London and then out into the country. The two girls played the game of bagging which house they would live in. They saw sheep, cows and horses. At the huge, empty halfway caféteria they each had a bun and a glass of orange. Back in the horrible smell of the coach it was Katie's turn to sit next to the window. At last they could see the great chalk barrier of the South Downs. As the coach passed through the white embankment they chanted: "When you see the sea you see the sea, see!" Indeed, it was coming nearer. They smelled it as soon as the door opened.

Aunty Betty and their cousins John and Doreen were waiting for them. Aunty Betty carrying the suitcases as they walked to the Steine. All over again Katie felt an excited love for this town, and the gardens, houses, sea and smelly pebbles. Everything here was so different to the dark houses of London in dull straight streets: here air and light ruled.

The number 96 trolley-bus was waiting and they went upstairs to the very front where they sat with their feet up on the front wall, driving a team of horses — this was a stage coach. The jerks and glides of the trolley bus took them up and up the long road that followed the scarp slope of the Downs towards the estate where Aunty Betty lived, towards the setting sun.

"If we could go faster," said Theresa, "we would always be in the sunshine."

The house was on a hill, so steep that the paving-stones were ridged to make them less slippery. Crossing the road to the small brick and tile semi-detached house, they entered through the front door which was at the side of the house and passed through a rather cold hall into a large carpeted lounge. There everything was modern, with two studio couches covered in red and black patterned moquette, some foam-cushioned chairs covered in similar fabric set out around a stone-faced fireplace with a gas fire. A large radiogram stood at the other end of the room and beside the door that led to the kitchen, a table and chairs.

The table had been laid. There were ham sandwiches and cakes with bowls of tinned peaches and a jug of evaporated milk to follow. Aunty Betty made her own cakes. Katie ate with relish, Theresa picked at a sandwich but ate the peaches with lots of milk quite quickly.

"Well, how's your mother?"

"She's very well, thank you."

"Are you all getting on all right? It must seem strange not to have Uncle Robert any more, but it was all for the best that he passed on. No one wants to stay alive if they're so very ill. . . . I've put you and Theresa to sleep with Doreen and John in the back room. I'm afraid it will be a bit crowded. Gordon can keep his little room. Come on, then, we'll take your suitcases upstairs. Your mother wrote to me. She said that you had an envelope for me."

Katie immediately wished that she had mentioned the envelope first. Maybe it sounded as though she might not be meaning to give it to her aunt.

"Yes, Aunty Betty. I meant to say it's in the little case. I'll fetch it now." She rose to go into the hall. She felt quite full up with the tea.

11

Her aunt sat on the beach. John, Theresa and Katie either went swimming or took their spending money to the Palace Pier. For a penny a go, they viewed the drunkard's dream, the haunted house and other mechanical wonders. Every day they could afford an ice cream, a better buy than the candyfloss, which looked so great but tasted of nearly nothing. At the far end of the pier, for sixpence, they could pass a horrible laughing mechanical clown in a glass case and enter a maze of distorting mirrors with many doors, some false, which might lead to a blank wall or not open at all. At the end of a dark and purple passage was a blacklined room and it was here that the Great Blondini performed his magic, when at least two or three members of an audience could be gathered together.

The Great Blondini entered a tiny pool of light and threw his long black cloak into the shadows, revealing himself magnificent in leopardskin trunks that extended up and over one shoulder. Instantly he would disappear, to return bearing a box on legs from which he withdrew two razor blades and a sheet of paper which he proceeded to slice into shreds with first one and then the other blade. He ate the blades, which could be distinctly heard crunching in his mouth. He gave the impression of enjoying a sticky toffee, which, with a great gulp, he swallowed and the blades were gone, in proof of which he opened a big empty mouth. Next, from his box, he took an electric light-bulb, crushed it under a black-booted foot, and then, crouching, enjoyed eating it. It took him three mouthfuls to consume and three great gulps to swallow. From behind the black curtain he brought in a board covered in nails. He carried it over to the three children and, although Theresa refused, the other two touched the points sticking out towards them. Placing the board on the floor, he very carefully lowered himself to a sitting position on it, then stretched full out and lay stiffly, only his head and the part of his legs below the knees not on the nails. After a few seconds he rolled sideways and sprang up, his arms in the air, towering over the seated trio. They failed to clap.

Realizing their mistake as he walked away, they moved a little uneasily on their seats. He ate fire, looked like the devil and, as a finale, lifted weights on an iron pole. It was an effort but he managed it, dropped them back again with a crash, bowed and left. Katie herself tried the weights but was unable to shift them, felt her arms stretching and her shoulders and back pulling, realized it was hopeless and gave up the attempt. The man from the box-office came and told them to leave now, handing John a sheet of paper. Outside in the light they read that on the fourth of August the Great Blondini was to jump into the sea, bound in ropes and chains, from the end of the pier.

The next day John did not want to see Blondini again, so Theresa and Katie went through the maze and sat by themselves waiting for the man to appear. He seemed to recognize them as soon as he entered. The act was exactly the same as before and it did not seem necessary to clap. After the final crash and the bow, they left well satisfied.

The man in the box-office also knew them from the previous day. "If you come again," he told them with a smile, "you can go in for threepence." They rushed off to tell their aunt the wonderful news.

After that they went every day. Sometimes other

people were there. When there was clapping the sisters clapped louder and longer than any of the others.

At night in bed, while it was still light outside, they discussed their hero. Theresa started to chant: "The great Blondini! The great Blondini!"

"You be quiet and go to sleep up there, or I'll come up and smack you all, do you hear?" called Aunty Betty from the bottom of the stairs.

They waited until they heard the door downstairs close. In a whisper Doreen said, "My Mummy says that she feels sorry for you, Katie."

This was interesting; they waited.

"She says that when you were born you were the apple of your Dad's eye but when Theresa was born he ignored you and only liked her. She said that she felt really sorry for you."

How had Katie not noticed? It must be true if Aunty Betty said so. Katie had been told that when the war was on she had gone to stay with her Granny in Wales but she did not remember that either. Neither did she remember the war. There was a big blank in her life.

"Uncle Robert was married before, wasn't he, Katie? And then she died. You were named after her. My Mummy was married to my real father before she married Tony. . . . When I grow up I only want to be married once. Do you, Katie?"

And Katie thought that if Mummy was their real mother, why had Daddy married before? Could she have been their mother as well? But she replied:

"I want to live in the country and be married to a farmer, I suppose. I don't like boys very much."

"You! Take your pyjamas down and I'll let you see my sausage," said John.

He was about a year younger than Katie. She did not think he was very clever, but he looked nice and she quite liked him, for a boy. She had seen them before, under the table in the infants class, all the boys wiggies — silly funny things — and in turn they had asked to see hers. But if you pulled your knickers aside there was nothing there to see. Pulling her trousers down, she kneeled on top of the bed. John stood up on his bed and pulled his trousers down. It was like a deformity, that wrinkled pink lump and the soft sausage hanging down in front. Poor boys, she thought, if they all had this.

12

After a morning on the beach and the ritual worship of the strong man, they packed and left to have lunch with Uncle Tony, who worked for the Post Office and was a bit frightening, with a deep grating voice and skin that was very brown, although his hair was almost white. Katie had a vague fear that at any minute he might laugh or say something savage, but the cousins seemed to really like their stepfather.

On the street near the Post Office was a restaurant where upstairs a waitress served everyone fish and chips. It was a wonder to see plates piled high with crinkly hot fried fish and a mound of chips, plates of bread and butter and cups steaming with sweet tea. Salt and vinegar sat on the table, free to all. This must be the best food in the whole world, Katie thought, filling her mouth with chips.

Looking around the room, she saw him — it was him, in the corner on his own. She was suddenly unable to chew or to swallow. She tried to balance the chips from her mouth on to the fork, which shook so much in her hand that the chips were strewn over the table.

"Your eyes are bigger than your tummy," said Uncle Tony.

"Yes, eat your food properly! If you don't want it, just leave it on the plate," said Aunty Betty.

He heard nothing of all this, nor had he seen her. He was reading his newspaper propped up in front of his plate. Katie could see shoulders, usually so strong, creasing a mid-grey suit. He wore a white shirt and a rather bright purple tie. Only his hair was still in the same style, blond, with a quiff in the front, though now she noticed what she had not seen in the darkened arena, that it was greasy — Brylcreem, she supposed. She thought, tenderly, that he was right to present a modest appearance out here in the world. A man as strong and clever as he was need not make a show of himself. She would like to be with him, although she did not like it at all when people looked at her, because she really wanted to be ordinary. But when you had a father who was different...it was difficult. Her throat jerked. *She had been disloyal again.* The chips now looked dry-coated and the tea had a layer of paleness on it. *Please don't let me cry.* Katie put her hands over her face, but through a tiny gap she could see him sipping tea and still looking at the paper. *Look at me! Let's run away together.*

She saw him leave, then return, but only to collect his paper from the table. Now Katie felt better and almost hungry again. Her aunt said that she should not get any ice-cream because she had not eaten her dinner but she did have some.

Sitting on the beach during the afternoon, Katie dreamily turned the pebbles over, looking for some treasure. This was being in love, she thought. *I would run away with him. I would do anything that he asked and if he wanted it I could do it without being asked. I can cook some things, clean and wash up. Perhaps I don't wash clothes very well, but I could run away.*

Without closing her eyes she had a very clear picture of him sitting there in the restaurant all alone. Being alone was a very funny thing because in some ways it was easier to be alone — you could wander about and think what you liked and that was nice. But in another way it was very frightening when people looked at you and then you felt as if you might do something wrong and bad things could happen and you should not talk to strangers — but they were only people, and you had to say things to people, sometimes, even if you did not know them.

If only she had been able to see Ursula again before she left, but she could not get away because her mother had said that she must stay and help her with the shopping before they went to the seaside. She had asked God to wait, please, not to decide yet if her father was bad, because it was not true and she would do anything — she would cut off her arm if He wanted her to — to make up for any deficiencies. It must be possible to arrange for her father and for her to be saved. God wanted them to be good and He had shown He was kind: no one had found out that she had not been at school for one afternoon; no one had seen when she took a cigarette from Aunty Emily's bag; she had not lost anything for a long time and she was helping Aunty quite a lot and being good.

Again Katie pictured Blondini sitting sipping his tea, looking at his newspaper. Her heart felt like custard.

"Please can I go and buy a postcard to send to Mummy?"

"Yes, but only along the front, don't go across the road. I don't think your mam would appreciate a dirty postcard."

The children laughed at this but Katie felt hurt and protective towards her mother, who was certainly the best woman in the world and ought not to be associated with smut.

She walked along the path alongside the beach and past the shops that lurked darkly under the promenade; some stank of onions while others were walled in by sugary goods, looking like the house in "Hansel and Gretel". Nearly level with the ramp that led up to the upper road was a stall selling souvenirs and in front of that a rotating rack of picture postcards. She found the best one, bearing five small pictures, all very pretty, of different parts of Brighton. She removed it from the rack and then added another from the top section, reserved for other pictures, not just views. This picture of a beautiful horse's head she would send to Christine. The cards in her hand, she walked over to the stall and was looking at the sunglasses and skull keyrings when she nearly bumped into a man hardly taller than herself, with a big nose and twinkly eyes.

"Hello, young lady, and what can I do for you?" he said.

"Well, now. Good afternoon, Miss. You're out shopping this afternoon without your little sister, I see." The man from the pier appeared from behind the stall and was standing beside the little man.

"So you know this young lady, Harry?"

"This lovely young lady is one of our best customers. Isn't that right, my dear?"

"Yes," Katie replied, blushing a bit.

A silence followed and she went on looking at the novelties, thinking that perhaps she should say something. She looked up to find that he was still looking at her.

"I think he is very brave," Katie said.

The man from the pier looked puzzled, then smiled and laughed. "You like him, do you? My name's Harry. What's yours?"

"Katie."

"Why don't you come in here, Katie, and I'll show you a very handsome man. You'll like him."

"Do you think you ought to?" asked the other man.

"This young lady's a friend of mine, aren't you?

You wait out here, Jack. Come on, Katie, you'll like this."

She took his hand and walked around the banked-up stall into the narrow passage behind. She noticed a rubbery smell and saw high shelves piled up with beach shoes and swim-hats. Harry sat on a chair that filled the end of the space. He was unfastening a small white cardboard box.

"Come on over here. You'll have to sit on my lap because there isn't another chair."

She liked sitting there. He felt warm and had a friendly aroma of tobacco. He put his arm around her and gave her a squeeze, quite hard.

"Ouch!"

He laughed and went on unwrapping the thing in the box. He had in his hand a rubber toy — a model Scotsman — which made her smile. Her face was very near his cheek, looking hard and bumpy with little hairs sprouting through.

"Now just watch this . . . . " He pressed the toy and the rubber kilt lifted up in the front as a pink rubber sausage-like piece pushed at it. She laughed with surprise. He squeezed her round the waist again. "I knew you'd like it, didn't I say so?"

His hand on her knee was going up and down the top part of her leg, she did not really mind but she wanted to go. She felt too hot and she had seen a rude toy. That was enough. She felt his chest heaving against her side. She wriggled to stand up.

"Just stay there for one minute, there's a good girl. Pretend that you're my little girl and I'm your Daddy. You love your Daddy, don't you?"

"Yes."

Katie gently put her arm around his neck to wait for the minute to end. He clutched and then released the side flesh of her waist. She felt his other hand on the inside of her leg and then she felt something — she knew that it was not a hand, and it seemed very hot. His hand propelled it up and down against her leg. She pulled sharply away but the hand clutched her.

He sounded angry. "No! Don't move! Stay still."

She sat rigid while he shuddered and sweated. She felt a hot sticky fluid on her leg and pushed hard against his shoulder to be free of him. She made a step forward but he grabbed her hand and pulled her back.

Again he sounded angry. "Don't go away. Now wait!"

He pulled a handkerchief from his trouser pocket. Katie noticed that the buttons of his trousers were undone. He wiped her leg, rubbed the hanky across his nose and put it back in his pocket. Again she went to leave but he pulled her back, this time sounding firm rather than angry.

"Now you won't tell anyone about this, will you? No one at all. Not even your Mummy, your Daddy or your sister. Do you understand?"

She nodded.

Then he sounded kind again. "Here's two shillings to buy some ice cream, and you can come to see the show whenever you like without paying — that's as long as you keep our little secret. All right?"

Katie sighed and nodded again. He made no move to stop her as she turned and left.

"Katie, you're bright red.... You've been a long time. What on earth have you been up to?"

She suddenly recalled that she had gone to buy picture postcards and now she had returned without any. How could she buy one now? And yet she had promised to send one to her mother.

"I've been running," she replied. Well, she had

run a tiny bit on the way back.

"You're a funny little girl, Katie. Where's that card for your mother?"

Katie was sure that her aunt would come to know somehow, would find out about the dirty things and she was afraid that the florin would fall out of her pocket when everyone knew that she only had a shilling.

Her aunt was laughing. Aunty Betty was funny, different from Mummy, more frightening. She would snap at you more but she would suddenly stop and be funny, as if she was enjoying herself, like now. What a relief!

Katie stretched out on her back, loving the feel of the hard pebbles; but the smell of the rubber, the tobacco and the man seemed to cling to her. She believed that it was not literally so — that would have been a problem. *But how can you wash inside your head, all your insides?* That was impossible — unless God could forgive you. Aunty Betty and her children did not go to church or pray, Katie had observed, and yet God did not seem to be punishing them.

At tea, Katie became rather afraid to eat because of a suspicion that her aunt might be poisoning her food. Food always tasted different away from home, but really the teatime food did have a strange taste. Becoming more convinced that it was indeed poisoned, she speculated on a means to warn her sister but in truth was more afraid of ridicule or being told off (Theresa couldn't be trusted not to tell on you) than even of Theresa dead. She knew that she would really regret it like when Daddy died. However much she reasoned and understood the right way to go, she could not make herself do it. *I will become strong enough to learn the hard way.*

Now the milk was tasting strangely normal.

13

After Brighton, where the light washed over everything almost to the point of haziness, even the trees in London revealed more profound colours: like looking at an oil painting after a day in a gallery of watercolours. For Katie, coming home was like a new careful look at a familiar picture. For a change, she saw her own home clearly. All the edges and objects that normally were passed without notice now stood out, surreal on account of their familiarity. Mummy had moved lots of things but nothing was gone, or was it?

Katie ordered her sister to start arranging the model farm until she came back from a visit to the toilet, but, observing Theresa absorbed in the preliminaries to this game, Katie instead went upstairs to the little room, originally meant for a maid, that had been Daddy's study. Mummy said that one day Katie would have it as her own room. There was a double cupboard just inside the door, the bottom part of which contained the hot water tank; the top half was full of slatted wooden shelves. On a shelf, right at the back behind a pipe, stood a tin. Katie climbed on to a chair and, stretching as far as she was able, just managed to move the tin a little towards her and to grasp it between thumb and finger and draw it to her. She sat down on the bed. The big roll-top desk and the drawing-board had gone and now the room seemed empty, the wall looked bare with only the gas bracket curling out like a twig in winter. This had provided light long ago before electric lights. Still, if you turned the tap gas came out; it smelt nice.

Inside the old tobacco tin she found the whole cigarette that she had stolen from Aunty Emily, plus two dogends she had found in the house, the papers that had belonged to Daddy and a box with four matches in it. All the cigarettes were crackly and dried out. She sniffed at each one in turn, put the whole one in her mouth; then, on hearing a sound on the stairs, she thrust all the bits into the tin and shoved the tin under the bed. Her mother was at the door.

"What are you doing in here, Katie? You've been in the airing-cupboard. You've ruckled up the bed. Go on, go downstairs."

There was nothing for it but to return downstairs. They made a big farm all over the floor of the conservatory. She had to stay at home that day because it was their first day back. After an hour or so, she became bored, wanting to go into the fresh air, the open space of the Common. It would be no use asking again. Christine and her family were away. The summer holiday had still a long way to go. Still, it would be nice to wake up each morning and know that there was no school.

By the second day back, she was allowed to go to the stables to see if they needed any help, her mother having grown tired of her restlessness at home. Katie was even given sandwiches for lunch. At the bottom of the hill she caught the 159 bus to Brixton Hill and made her way to the spiritualist house. The same man who had opened the door before opened it again this time.

"Hullo. Your name's Katie, isn't it?"

"Yes." She felt at ease and pleased. "Is Ursula here, please?"

"No, she's in Scotland for the summer. Do you want to come in?"

She entered the same room as before. The man returned with a glass of lemonade, then left her alone in the room. She drank her drink, which was welcome. Already it had become very warm, although it was only ten o'clock in the morning. She was just wiggling forward out of the deep, low chair to put the glass back on the table as the door opened to admit a young man wearing a grey suit with white stripes in the cloth, a white shirt with a very pretty blue tie. His face was pointed, birdlike, his hair a bit long, thick and curly, trained flat, but now beginning to stick up in the hot air.

He smiled at her, said, "Hello, I'm Michael," and then, giving his trousers a hoist at the knees, sat opposite her, his hands clasped together resting on his knees. He gazed at her steadily for a long time. She watched his shoulders going up and down with his regular breathing.

"Don't worry. I used to be worried. I used to have headaches and they stopped me working. Since I started to work in spiritualism I have felt very good." He shuffled a bit in the chair. He was looking over her shoulder, rocking his head, saying: "Yes. . . yes."

Then: "There is a man and there is a little baby. Do you know who they are, Katie? It is Katie, isn't it? Mm. . . they have passed over. They are very peaceful."

Katie felt strange, now that he was looking at her again, sitting so close that she could not look at him any longer. Instead she looked at the blue of his tie.

"Do you know who they are, Katie?"

"I don't know any dead babies, I don't know."

"Relax. Don't worry. I can only pass on what I see and hear. You understand, don't you?"

She nodded, still looking into the blue of his tie.

The man called Michael put his hands to his chest, which heaved up and down. "Someone who passed over had a bad chest. I can feel the pain. It's very uncomfortable, do you understand?"

It must be her father. *His* chest heaved — it was full of funny noises. She did not really want to say so. She nodded.

The young man smiled and nodded his head, "Yes. . . yes." Again he was looking past her. "I feel warmth. They send you love. You mustn't be sad. Sometimes it's better for people to pass over — it's beautiful in the spirit world. To stay in this world was too much suffering. Do you understand?"

Katie nodded. Now she wanted this to be over.

"There is an Indian. He watches over you and can help you. But only if you believe in him. Do you understand?"

There was a pause and then Michael continued: "You will have a full life. You will suffer, because you are a very sensitive person. Through your suffering you will gain understanding, will grow — I don't mean taller — I mean, you will grow into a person of knowledge who will be able to help other people."

She smiled politely at his face, which did not stop smiling back at her. He seemed a very kind person.

He leaned forward. "Does your mother know that you are here today?"

"Yes." *Another lie. I have spoiled even this place.*

"Good. Tell her that she would be very welcome at one of our meetings. They are on Wednesday evenings at 7.30 pm, and on Sundays at 11 o'clock in the morning and 6.30 pm. Most people find it a great comfort, even if they don't receive a personal message. I felt your spirits very near you this morning. I hope you didn't mind; it's my job. I am honoured to be able to pass on messages from the spirit world — it's very close to us, you know. There's nothing to fear."

Katie found herself biting her nails, not a thing

71

she usually did. "Thank you very much. My father had a bad chest, but I don't know any dead babies."

"One day it will fit. Don't try and make it — just bear it in mind. Remember that there's a lot of love for you. I can feel it."

Outside, the air felt very warm and sparrows chirped in the knobbly lime trees, bent like huge arthritic limbs out of the tiny front gardens. She pondered her recent experiences as she walked along. She had not sensed any spirits. Now in the warm sunlight she did not want to feel different. She wanted to go somewhere and lie on the grass, to be a Gulliver among the blades, to feel all her body as it pressed against the ground. That never felt bad.

14

When Katie arrived at the shop, a strong smell of frying from the back room reminded her that it was lunchtime. Ann's head appeared from behind the curtain.

"Oh, it's you, Katie. Come on through."

Katie felt a strength and warmth surge through her. She felt so grown up. Was Ann aware, that in the simplest things she was offering something as precious to Katie as gold? The room was full of fumes.

"Would you like a fried egg and some fried bread, or have you eaten?"

Oh, dear. Katie remembered leaving her paper bag of sandwiches beside the chair in Brixton — they would ring her mother and there would be an awful lot of trouble. She had told so many fibs. Maybe Michael had known all along and that was why it had not worked. It had seemed ordinary and she had been unable to look at him. Her heart sank. The feeling of joy should have been a warning, she realized.

"Do you want this?" Ann was holding a plate with a broken egg on it, beside which lay a piece of fried bread, not even and golden like Mummy's, but darker brown with bits of burnt crumbs from the pan sticking to it. She took the plate, but her appetite did not return. Nevertheless she ate it all. When Katie had nearly finished, Ann started to eat her own lunch.

"How was your holiday?"

"It was very nice, thank you. We went to Brighton." It seemed a hundred years ago now.

"I haven't been there for ages. It's difficult to get around much with the dogs and the shop. When

73

you've finished, go and see if I've turned the sign to Closed. I expect I forgot. Let's have our cup of tea in peace."

This tea tastes better than Mummy's or Granny's, thought Katie; *maybe because it's from a mug.* When the liquid was finished Katie spooned some sugar from the bottom. She looked at Ann, who was busy reading the *Daily Mirror*.

"Please, may I take Jason out for a walk?"

"He'd like that. He hasn't had a good walk for ages. You know where the leads are kept."

Whether or not Jason actually liked the idea of a walk, it was rather embarrassing to have to drag him out of the shop and along the pavement. Once he got used to the idea, he pulled on ahead. Halfway up the Common, where the grass was still smooth, Katie stretched out on her stomach. She could not let Jason run free and it was difficult to lie still and peaceful because he kept standing up, ready to move on. Dogs in films were children's best friends — they curled up and slept alongside them.

The cosy thought reminded Katie of her little sister in a pram with the hood up, Theresa all snug and lovely inside, while outside it was raining. . . Katie had been jealous. *Babies. . . who was that baby?* Daddy had a baby with him, the medium had said. Was that other woman there too? If they had been together, shining side by side, surely the man Michael would have told her.

Katie lifted herself out of the grass. She did not want to go home yet; she wanted to go to the toilet, so she walked, Jason pulling her towards the top of the Common. Beside the café were two passages marked by metal rails and dark overhanging laurels, each with their own sign pointing the direction for Ladies or Gentlemen to take. She tied Jason's lead to the metal railing between the two signs. The brass box on the door clunked back and swallowed the penny piece down. When she returned along the shaded passage, Jason was sitting patiently waiting. She patted his head, aware of the gaze of passers-by on her and her beautiful dog. Katie joined the queue of people waiting to enter the café, checking several times that her threepenny bit was in her pocket under the hankie. As she neared the doors she had decided on the forthcoming lolly: it was to be a tuppenny one, long on a stick, blackcurrant; if sucked hard enough it came out white ice.

Leaving the café, she had only time for a tiny suck at the ice before observing that the place where the dog had been tied to the railings was now bare. A small crowd stood in the road. In a daze she walked through them and there on the road flat on his side was Jason, his lead stretched out over the tarmac. She hesitated at the edge of the crowd, wanted to walk away, was overcome by a surge of feelings. Without a thought for the people, she dropped her ice, ran forward and knelt beside the animal. His eyes were closed and there was some pee coming out of his bottom. A man came forward and stood beside her as she gently stroked the dog's cheek, tears rolling down her face.

"We must get him to a vet," said the man.

The man, Katie and a woman lifted the dog on to the back seat of a car parked nearby. The dog filled the seat, its paws touching the backs of the front seats. Katie took the passenger seat and the woman seated herself to drive. They went first to the police station, Katie kneeling on the seat stroking the dog and crying. While the woman was in the police station, the dog's eyes opened and he made a move to rise but decided to lie still, or perhaps he had no strength. Katie felt a little hopeful as Jason looked at her.

"Shh, shh. It's all right, you'll be all right." It had to be true.

The woman had driven to a house and fetched the vet out with her. While the dog tried to get up, they all carried him in and put him on a table covered in rubber sheeting. The dog sat up and then the vet had him on his feet, now Jason wanted to jump off the table. The vet's hands went all over the dog's body, then pulled the bottoms of his eyelids down and looked in. Katie and the woman had trouble holding Jason as the vet stuck a thermometer up his bottom. The vet was nice and spoke to Jason all the time in a very comforting tone. At the end of the examination he lifted the dog off the table and gave Katie the lead to hold. He went to a cupboard and poured some white pills from a large brown jar into a small white envelope which he handed to Katie.

"He's had a nasty knock on the head, poor old chap. Take him home, give him one of these every four hours and leave him in a very quiet dark place to rest. He'll be all right. Go on giving him the pills tomorrow."

Jason was pulling to go and leapt into the back seat of the car where Katie climbed in to sit beside him. She had her arms around him and kissed his shoulder. The woman came out to the car and said yes, she knew where the pet shop was and she stopped the car right outside. Katie and Jason rushed in — Katie anxious to fetch Ann out to see the woman — but by the time Ann had come out the car had driven off.

The shop was already closed at half-past six and so they sat in the back while Katie told Ann of the afternoon's events. She gave her the dog's pills. Jason was busy eating some chopped red meat. He looked as if nothing at all had happened to him.

"I am so sorry, Katie," said Ann finally.

It is me who should be sorry, thought Katie, feeling overcome both by the kindness of the woman who had saved Jason and now by Ann's easy forgiveness.

"You'd better wash your face before you go home." She handed Katie a dirty towel. Katie cleaned her face off in the sink, above the plates and the mugs left piled there after lunch.

"I don't suppose you'll want me to take Jason out tomorrow, but if you do I shall be very pleased."

"I'm sorry I'm so late," she said when she came home.

"Where on earth have you been to? I rang the stables and they said that you hadn't been there all day."

Katie made an effort on her mother's behalf to look more repentant.

"I went to the pet shop instead." She recounted the events of the afternoon to her mother, who said that everyone had been very kind. Katie wondered if at any minute her mother was going to say that the spiritualists had telephoned her, but instead she was told to go and put on her pyjamas before tea. It still remained light until late in the evening and so going upstairs did not matter.

She undressed in the bedroom and did not even mind going to bed when it was light this once. The birds sang outside a reflection of her happy thankfulness. Sad things, bad things and happy things were all mixed up: her head was spinning. *What is it like to suffer? I know I am not really brave.* Katie prayed for everyone to be better and thanked God for her luck. Eventually she was asleep.

15

About four times a year they took bus rides across London to visit their more important friends. Mrs Levy was doubly important. First, she was a Jew. Katie's mother had a great admiration for the chosen people. "Jesus was a Jew," she would tell them. Furthermore Mrs Levy was an educated woman — a child psychiatrist. To Katie she was rather frightening, ugly and fat. Her flat had a strange smell, probably of foreign food. Katie had a feeling that Mrs Levy did not like them all that much. Seeming too clean and very English, they sat in her dark flat, full of pictures and ornaments, a place that could never be properly cleaned. Even the tea tasted funny but the biscuits were very nice with soft jammy centres, called stuffed monkeys.

Mrs Levy left them to go into her tiny kitchen and returned with a creased screw of greaseproof paper. "Would you like a black olive?"

By coincidence, only the week before Katie had read of black olives. Some princess, foreign, maybe Persian, had been quoted in *John Bull* magazine as saying that black olives were her favourite food. Now the moment had come when Katie could feel part of a most exotic world set, the people who ate black food.

"I adore black olives," she said, quoting directly from *John Bull*.

Her mother gave a start and just managed to stop herself asking her daughter if she really wanted one of the disgusting-looking grey, shrivelled, shiny things sitting on the paper in front of them. Mrs Levy smiled and indicated that she should eat.

Katie was revolted by the touch of the thing but the taste was even worse. Indeed, there must be something wrong, unless it was some kind of test. These things, or at least this one — though they all looked similar — must have gone bad. There was nothing for it but to pretend that this was the most delicious delicacy the world had to offer. She would die for her sins, Katie was convinced, as she chewed and swallowed, remembering to smile. Finally it was over and she placed the stone back on the paper. Her pretence had worked too well and she found herself eating a second. Definitely she did not belong in the company of foreign princesses. A wave of affectionate understanding with her mother passed through her mind. She was prepared to die this lie through — *die lying, lie dying*.... Katie became aware of strength as obstinance and misdirected. As she drank a second cup of tea, she wanted to be sick, but smiled, while her mother commented that olives were an acquired taste. Slowly she felt better and almost immediately felt her good resolutions betrayed by a desire to acquire new tastes.

Her mother stood up, with a glance at Mrs Levy, and started to pile up the empty cups and saucers, though when Katie made a move to help with the biscuit plate she said: "No, dear, Theresa can help Mummy." The door to the kitchen closed behind them. The sound of running water and the chink of china were the only noises.

Mrs Levy rose from the sofa, crossed in front of the rows and rows of books, took a cigarette out of a box almost lost among the ornaments on the bottom shelf of the bookcase, lit a cigarette and returned to the table. Katie would have liked to try smoking a cigarette.

"Do you miss your father?" There were other questions about dreams, school, her fears.

Katie had polite falsehoods for all occasions. She

felt she could tell lies for ever and ever and it no longer mattered. She made up a story, which she said was a dream, about men who lived in lampposts:

"They make babies cry — they go out and pinch babies — otherwise they just eat worms and things that grow around garages and places. They don't do much really. They're quite thin." She added the last fiction, thinking how fat Mrs Levy seemed.

Did Mrs Levy know it was all a lie? Once started, it was easy to tell fibs. They could grow and grow and anyway no one could know what she dreamed when she was asleep. And Mrs Levy seemed interested.

Finally Mrs Levy went to the kitchen door and opened it. "Oh, my dear! You've done all the washing up. You really shouldn't have done that. Thank you so much! Come and sit down — I've been having a very interesting talk with Katie."

Katie smiled at her mother and her mother smiled at Katie.

16

"Do you really love black olives, darling? Did you have them at Aunty Betty's? Would you like me to see if I can buy some at the shops this morning?"

"No, it's all right. I don't really want any right now. It was just nice to have them yesterday."

"Oh, yes. Well. . . by the way, what did you and Mrs Levy talk about?"

"She wanted some stories that happen in dreams. Nothing much, really."

Katie looked down at her bread and marmalade. She had heard her mother speaking to Mrs Levy on the telephone just before breakfast. Perhaps she did not believe Mrs Levy, or maybe she was checking up to see if her daughter was truthful. *But there are such things as secrets, which are like lies.* Who could know . . ? Who was that woman in the photograph? *Maybe Mummy is not really my mother; maybe even my father wasn't real; who can tell?* Sometimes things seemed so real and sometimes they seemed so unreal; even the best things, the stories in the Bible, could make you wonder. *It is easy to be wrong because you aren't brave enough, but then God is forgiving.* Sometimes people seemed to do bad things and be good, and others were trying to be good but they weren't right. In some ways it all made sense and in other ways, by not trying, it was easier. All saints and martyrs had suffered, although bad people had to suffer too. By now it had become clear to Katie that there really was no way of knowing.

"It's not like you to take no interest in your food. Do you feel all right?"

"I've got a tummy ache."

"Stay in while we go shopping. It will do you good to stay at home instead of roaming around the

Common or hanging about those stables. I don't expect Miss Foster needs you to help her. We won't be long. Clear up the breakfast things."

Katie kissed her mother and her little sister. It seemed an important thing to do, like the time after Daddy died, when everything had been so intense between them. Mummy seemed pleased and looked so beautiful as they left.

Alone in the house, at first Katie felt very important. She cleared up very well. Then there was a gap. She did not want to go out; she did not want to look at her mother's bedroom; she did not want to paint or to play or to make anything. She walked around and looked into every room, knowing every item everywhere.

In her father's study she sat on the bed. *When it's my room I'll have two walls grey and two walls red, in comtemporary wallpapers.* Wallpapers were like the new exercise books at the beginning of term when the new pages were so lovely. By the end of term the books were full of mistakes and ugly. She could imagine this room looking so lovely, but now here she was staring at the cupboard and thinking about the cigarettes. The room always stank of Woodbines when Daddy worked here. With some difficulty she retrieved the tin. After one half of the crackling smoky cigarette her head was swirling. She hid the evidence, sensing that things were wrong, and, before lying back on the bed, she turned the tap on the gas bracket a half-turn so that the tap followed the line of the tube and unblocked the flow of gas. Why didn't the tube swell up and burst under the pressure of all that gas? *Oh, yes, I must try and see and believe in the Indian. Maybe I am very close to the Indians; they are all round-faced, almost featureless like me and, like me, they love horses and nature. I'll just be a bit nearer Daddy.*

The cigarette had made her feel ill but she quite liked the smell of the gas. there was that funny buzzing sound and the flashes inside her eyes and Katie felt herself, heard herself, in an echoing tunnel, like at the dentist's. *In a minute I will turn off the gas. Mummy will be coming home. . . .*

BLACK STOCKINGS

Day One

I have decided to write this diary. I will write it between ten o'clock and ten-thirty every night. I have a friend who finishes his work in a restaurant at ten. From ten until maybe eleven I usually cannot concentrate on anything because I am wondering if he is going to come and see me. I hope that by keeping a diary I will fill in this time, instead of just sitting and waiting. Also it may help me to see if there is any pattern to my feelings, which seem to change from day to day for no discernible reasons. If there is no pattern, that will be something learnt.

He is Pasquale. He is my boyfriend — which is rather a silly title. I do not like the name Pasquale; it is only one better than Pepe, which must be the silliest name in the world.

I live in a bed-sitting-room. I deliberately keep it very plain. The floor is grey lino, the walls are white, the bedcover yellow and the curtains turquoise. A wardrobe hides the two big closed doors which lead to someone else's room on the other side. Two chairs have high wooden-slatted backs and cane seats. These chairs are set each side of the fireplace. Another chair, plain wood, fits under the Formica-topped table at which I now sit, beneath the window. Because this is the front room of the ground floor of a Georgian house the window has some elegance. The other touch of elegance in the room is the mantelpiece — perhaps I should say mantelshelf — anyway it is more neat than gaudy. The hearth is boarded in, with a gas fire placed on the maroon tiles, the meter around the corner of the chimney breast.

None of this room is my choice, but I approve of my landlord's taste. I have added just two personal

touches. On the mantelpiece is an old painted
Spanish jug, broken and mended with metal staples
long before I bought it. I liked it even more because
of its careful repairs. Above the mantelpiece I have
hung an abstract lithograph, grey, white and
turquoise coloured, framed in wood painted to look
like silvery metal. On the floor by the bed is a
radio/cassette-player, metal and plastic teak. I am
nearly addicted to the radio. I have six cassettes but
I am bored with them, and play only one —
selections from Tosca — when I am alone and
drunk.

I sometimes let the cat stay in here with me, he is
very lightweight and warm on my lap. He seems to
want to be my cat but I refuse to take responsibility
for him. The cat is not here now. Because of an
accident it seems as though there is another
creature in the room. It creeps along the lino — a
smooth-edged green-gold pool of olive oil. I have
watched it flowing slowly under the meter, around
the back leg of the chair, and now it is moving,
almost imperceptibly to get under the wardrobe. I
feel helpless to do anything to stop it.

Yesterday I cleaned the room. I had so much
energy then; in the end I stopped myself finding
more and more pernickety jobs — I almost
excavated the grime from the ribbed handle of the
radio/cassette with a toothpick. Tonight I just sit
here. Tomorrow morning, before I go to work, I
will clean up. I seem to have energy in the
mornings. Now is the time for waiting or a time for
carrying on with this new exercise — my diary.

It is ten-past ten and I have made myself a pot of
tea. The pot, brown and shiny, sits with a white
mug and a carton of milk on a metal tray. The tray
has lines of purple and white in a square design on
it, making it a temptation to arrange the objects in a

more geometric fashion.

The kitchen is at the back in the basement, shared by all the lodgers in the house, that is by six people. We also share a bathroom which is on my floor at the back above the kitchen. There is a pay phone on the landing between my floor and the first or top floor.

I somehow doubt that he will come tonight because last night we went out to a party. Often social events alienate us. We danced with other people and only once or twice together. I could see he watched me as I talked with others, and I watched him, coy but very charming, flirting with the women. I was not sure that he would take me home at one o'clock. I was drunk, tired and felt the need to avoid more noise and talk. I wanted some air, some peace and some sleep. He did drive me back. I went straight to bed. He sat for a while drinking whisky from a half-bottle he had brought with him. He smoked a cigarette — a sure sign that he has drunk too much — before joining me in the bed. What happened afterwards was so strong that, like a dream that is more powerful than the reality which follows, it has remained in my mind all today at work.

At about four o'clock I was woken up, in pain, Pasquale on top of me making love with no preliminary gestures at all. It occurred to me to protest but then the pain stopped and I began, in a sleepy way, to enjoy it. Then he hurt me again, he was buggering me, and I did protest, so that he finished in my vagina. I recalled that buggery is said to be the most common form of birth-control practised in Italy. When it was over, he just turned over with his back to me and went to sleep. I lay gazing at his back and loved him for his selfish act. I thought how content I would be if I could just be here and he would come and use me for his pleasure. But he would have to want me.... My doubts about that now have me sitting here feeling crabby. It is half-past ten.

The olive oil has reached a natural repose. I am full of contradictions: one day energetic, the next day hopeless. When asked for advice I am full of sound common sense, on the whole recommending activity, because in itself the results can be satisfying and also just the doing changes one's feelings. Yet I sit here. Do be, do be, do. Maybe it is some consolation that a year or so ago I would rush to the mirror at the onset of any crisis. Now I am reconciled to having mediocre looks. I also have a mediocre brain and I deliberately keep any soul-searching shallow. I have achieved a balance of thinking about breeding/upbringing/me being like other people yet different from them. It brings me the satisfaction of exhausting my powers of analysis.

I light a cigarette, the fifth today, the thousandth day of my life when I have sworn to give up. I like the feeling of nausea that smoking gives me. Sometimes I phantasize that I am pregnant, it is the sort of thing that some of my girl friends say, while I, on the whole, consider them a bunch of neurotic cows — a thought unfair to cows.

Day Two

Last night he did not come. It is now quarter-past ten. I sit here towards the end of one of those days when everything, for the time being, fits the facts: I have eaten sensibly, have maintained a choice of clean clothes, a sufficiency of cash, caught buses and arrived neither too late nor too early. In this repetition of the ordinary business of my life I have, in fact, been comfortably successful. Now I have come to the end of this day and even some part of tomorrow is looked after, for my morning's clothes are set out on a chair, but there is a gap until I can begin tomorrow. Probably I should go to bed and just sleep, but I feel energetic for something more. Maybe it is music that has stirred me, as I have just listened to Beethoven's Seventh Symphony on the radio. Anyway I want him to come, I want to talk to him, to touch him. Because he did not come last night it is slightly more probable that he will show up tonight. . . .

I carried the cat outside and walked up the street with it hugged in my arms, the sky was like shot-silk, gold and aubergine.

Today I read a whole book at work. I work in a shop. The shop sells expensive shirts, ties, sweaters and other accessories to rich men, or for them, to rich women. We also sell things to the charming or hard-bitten *nouveau riche*. I earn in a week about what a single one of the sweaters costs. Often someone will spend in less than half an hour what it takes me a month to earn. I have no feelings, beyond our shared business dealings, about these people, except that I sometimes feel sorry for those ones that suffer from a terrible need to acquire more and more clothes. Poor things — both the goods and the people.

I wear jeans or trousers, a shirt and a sweater (if it is cold) as a uniform — all of them nondescript enough to go together and be anonymously acceptable: they are usually clean. My boss, the owner of the shop, is a beautiful and gay young man. I never see him before lunch time unless he pops in to take some money before a lunch date with persons of fashion. He usually stays for a while during the afternoon. I open the shop and I lock it up. I do the accounts, the banking and the cleaning. I am trustworthy. I take sandwiches for my lunch, nearly always the same: Prewitts's stone-ground wholemeal bread with margarine and cheddar cheese, occasionally a piece of fruit. I eat my lunch from a drawer in the counter so that I can hide it quickly and serve if someone comes in. If I want to go out to buy coffee, or something from the chemist, I can either ask someone we know to stay there or else I lock the door. For long periods I just sit alone surrounded by many images.

The shop is lined with mirrors and with both transparent and dark-blue Perspex shelving (which attracts the dust). I have been reading Doris Lessing's books about Martha Quest, but, having finished the whole of *A Proper Marriage* today, I have grown a bit bored with the suburbs of South Africa. My boss is getting very excited about a party next Saturday. The principal of the event is to be Princess Margaret, with a chorus consisting of singers, dancers, designers, actors and certain royals, current and disused, who make up the gossip columns of the press. He says it is such a pity that I have to look after the shop, because otherwise I could go with him. He is always getting me to work on Saturdays and then easing his own guilt and my imaginary sorrow by telling me afterwards that I did not miss anything or that he was such a success that it was all worthwhile. It all seems about as real and boring as the suburbs of South Africa to me.

On the few occasions when I have met his fabled set I found that I bored them very quickly, rarely struck up interesting conversations, but like an old woman who once danced with the Prince of Wales, I

like to think that I have briefly rubbed shoulders
with these idols of our time.

Today was one of the quietest days I can
remember. It made my boss (I do not know why I
keep calling him "my boss", his name is Jeremy)
very uneasy. When the shop is busy he quickly gets
rather ratty with clients. Maybe they like it. He
only seems to find pleasure in his friends or people
he would like to be his friends. Besides himself, he
finds nearly everyone in the world tasteless. His
arrogance has undoubted charm and he is very
beautiful. I wonder what will become of him when
he is old and less pretty.

When, around teatime, I yawned he gave me a
pill. "These are marvellous, it will make you feel
good," he said. The pill made my mouth very dry
but I did feel quite chirpy. My suggestion that he
leave a supply of them in the shop he did not seem
to hear.

I went to see Elsie today. I can always be sure that
she will be at home when I call, because she suffers
from agoraphobia. She sat, as usual, next to the
kitchen table, her plump arms resting upon it. Her
uniform is a nylon overall covering an acrylic
sweater and Crimplene trousers, her chubby feet
bulge over the tops of button-down slippers, the
habitually made-up face and hair dull from years of
colouring and perms is framed by the upward-
curling patterns of smoke from her cigarette.

"Oh, it is lovely to see you, Katie. You don't know
how much I look forward to seeing you. . . I really
do. . . I don't know what I'd do without you. . . . Oh,
I'm so sorry."

She pushes out a chair from under the table for
me to sit down and hands me a cigarette, which I
accept. Then I ask her if she wanted any stuff from
the Greek before he closed. The list was lurking at

the bottom of the stiff brown plastic bag on the floor under the table. We went through the list: cigarettes from the newsagent, wine and gin from the off-licence, frozen carrots and peas (mixed) and nine tins of cat food from the Greek.

Outside a car has stopped and someone is coming up to the door. It is almost certainly Pasquale.

Day Three

Last night Pasquale arrived, carrying before him a case of wine. He tripped on the cat, nearly dropping his precious burden. The quality the cat has for causing annoyance to people, I admire greatly; it amounts to genius. The other lodgers are reduced to mad rage within seconds of an encounter. Such an emotional response would take me an hour or so of hard work to achieve. Pasquale swore in fury at the animal and literally kicked it out from under his feet.

I opened the case and took two of the curvaceous bottles down to the fridge. We opened one bottle of Verdicchio and drank it quickly, he telling me that he could not stay because he was tired and had promised to help a friend at work tomorrow. This was the same friend he had worked with on other occasions in a film-processing laboratory. Besides, last night he had gone to a party. Anger and jealousy tightened inside me. I could not bring myself to say, "You might have phoned me." If he does not already know, I am not likely to change him with crabby words.

"Please don't go," I said. "You can sleep here."

He smiled. I wanted him to kiss me. It became like an important token that he should reach out and

94

touch me, kiss me. He did not sense it. Sometimes I wonder if he is gay. I recall how angry I was when he suggested that I was a lesbian, when we first met and I would not go to bed with him. I hated him for not touching me, hated him, but wanted to lean over to his chair and stroke his hair and kiss his face. When it is good, it is very very good, but horrid when bad.

I only want the good bits, then I wonder about the tension of it all. "What are you doing tomorrow night after work?"

He says that he is going to wait for someone to ask him to dinner. By then I am humourless enough to take it as a rejection — I cannot even see the threads of an invitation. Consequently I have sat here now for half an hour, it is half-past ten, empty without an appetite, and feeling sad. I smoke and have drunk half a bottle of wine.

Damn him, I will go to bed.

Day Four

He knocked on the door; I heard him coming, although it was nearly midnight. I went to the door with just a piece of printed cotton wrapped around me, native-style. We sat in chairs by the fire, after he had gone down to the fridge to fetch some wine.

"I don't like you wandering around the house with nothing on," he said. "Do you have another man? Or do you just want another? I saw you dancing with Piero on Sunday. He was holding you very close."

Piero is a fifty-year-old balding barman, but I did not find the accusation amusing.

"I have told you so often, so why don't you

believe me? If I want another lover I will tell you. Do you feel guilty? Why are you always going on with this false jealousy? I have just one lover. There is only one man that I want."

"Who is he?"

I cannot believe that he is serious, but nevertheless I say: "His name is Pasquale."

He does not smile, he shakes his head.

"It was you who went off to a party on Monday without telling me."

Really I had not meant to say it. Whenever he is in the wrong I have to suffer. I used to like it, this complete lack of logic. Whenever he failed I had to suffer to save the day. Now I am tired of it. I used to like the fact that any suffering I felt was not registered at all. It made a refreshing change to anything I had known before.

"If I find you with another man I will kill you both. Do you understand?"

"You are stupid to say such things. I don't know if I believe you. Anyway, the prisons are full of people who regret something they once did, for reasons that are no longer important to them."

"For me it is the most important thing not to be betrayed by a woman. Maybe I care too much. I can't help it. Italians are like that. I expect you think that we are uneducated. I mean it, I will kill you."

I hate these things he says. Maybe I am important to him, I really do not know. When we first met I was a stripper then and he was unemployed. He had been sort of impressed that I had once been a teacher, stupid man. I was touched that he wanted me — his girl friend — to stop being a stripper. And I gave it up with no regrets except that it was a very easy way to earn a living. I was never really a good stripper (if they exist I do not know because I have never seen any in the West End). I worked in a local pub. Three nights a week and Sunday lunchtime. If I had any style it might be called puzzling. I was never nervous and I was very slow. I used a cheap, shortened, recording of Ravel's *Pavane for a Dead Infanta*. I stood on the tiny wooden stage and took off a sequined bolero, a silky, long black dress and then a petticoat, a bra, a suspender belt, a pair of black stockings, and finally, a tiny pair of side velcro-opening lacy black pants, which were the only thing that I bought especially for the act. When it was over, to the dying bars of the music, I took a long black velvet cloak (a gift from my mother, who never knew that I stripped) and covered myself. I wore red lipstick, black eye make-up and pale cream on my face. As far as I can remember I never smiled, nor did I change my expression throughout.

It was after my act one Sunday lunchtime that I was first introduced to Pasquale. He was acquainted with the girl who used to work behind the bar. We spoke very little but were aware of each other. The others in the group made some fun of Italians — spaghetti-eaters, good company but otherwise cowards, good for nothing except crime and eating and making large families and generally enjoying themselves, etc. Of course I felt sorry for him. He looked much more together than the other men present. He always wears very neat jeans or cord trousers, an immaculate shirt and has a talent for carrying a sweater over his shoulders, around his waist or his neck, and sometimes even wearing it properly. He had, I thought, heard all this stuff time and time again. I said little, anyway I always felt aloof at that bar. Maybe I was distanced because everyone had seen me with no clothes on, although none of them knew me well. But I never felt uneasy. When I left, he followed me outside and asked if I would have dinner with him the following Tuesday, which I accepted and felt quite pleased.

When things are bad, it is my experience that couples resort to reminiscing, and we are no exception. We recalled for the twentieth time how on first meeting we both wanted to be alone and go to bed together.

"I haven't changed, Katie," he said.

After English intellectuals who came alive only at the mention of depression, I welcomed the flow of words, the ease with which we quarrelled, and fell apart, were reconciled and together again. Now it had become a ritual and it was boring. Our shows of strength had once held me spellbound, strong is real, a throwback to half-forgotten parental rows that had me dancing with pleasure through a kaleidoscope of emotions. Last night, as I looked down at the grey lino, I wanted him to stay, or to go, but not to go on talking. Instead we went on drinking, which made him more moody. I tried coaxing him into a jollier frame of mind and then gave up.

Tonight I ate a tin of tuna with some vinegar on it and a slice of Prewitt's bread. I have drunk three-quarters of a bottle of wine and smoked about ten cigarettes. I feel sick. When I drink I always smoke too much, it is my preferred taste. "Barman, mix me a nausea!"

He said that he will come, so I suppose that he will — he has never failed to keep his word, although he can be very late. It is now eleven o'clock.

Day Five

When he arrived I was feeling drunk and sick. He

98

did not believe me, and I did not care. I sat at the table, he sat by the fire. I offered to fetch him a glass for some wine.

"Bring me some bread."

"Would you like some salami? I've got some. Or some cheese? Or some salad?"

"Some bread and a glass."

I went down into the kitchen, realizing that I would usually refuse such a dogmatic request. However, I did not care, so I came back up with the bread on a plate. I handed him the glass and put the bread on the table. He already had a bottle opened in one hand. I sat in the chair opposite him.

"Where's the bread?"

I got up thinking that I might let the bread slip on to the floor. Instead, I held the plate in front of him. He put his arms around me and pulled me down on to his lap. I just managed to put the plate on to the mantelpiece. I felt safe and contented and warm.

If a glimmer of a pattern is emerging, it is to expect the opposite. If events seem set fair, it is nearly certain that an unpleasant time will follow, whereas if it seems likely that things are going to be sticky, in fact, pleasant things are waiting in store.

He is not coming tonight, although he always adds that he might — just to see what I am up to. He claims to know what I do always, to know whom I see when I am not with him. Sometimes, even, it seems to be true. His uncle is arriving from Italy and after work he wants to see him. I always believe what he tells me. I got off the bus at the Angel tonight, thinking that I might see him for a minute or two as he started his work. I hung about opposite the restaurant for a while without catching a glimpse of him and then I decided to go home without going to find him. The walk made me feel fine.

I called in on Elsie, who is fretting about the rent officer coming. I have a list of things to buy her tomorrow, including dye for her hair which is artificially auburn. She is also worried because on Monday she has to go to the doctor's. For such a major expedition her husband will have to take her himself, in a taxi.

I have eaten baked beans and a slice of bread, washed up everything from today and last night and had a coffee with the West Indian recording engineer who lives in the room behind mine. He showed me a record cover that featured a picture of him pretending to play a trumpet. We listened to the disc, a very pleasant soft jazz for people who do not really like or know jazz. I told him that I had loved the word jazz when I was a child, ages before I had heard a note of the music. When I finally heard some real jazz I had hated it but had pretended that I loved it, of course. Now I have genuinely acquired the taste. He told me that when he first came to England he became engaged to two girls at the same time. The way he told the story made me feel that something of the sort was still going on. His room is full of shelves held up on bricks. The shelves are filled with long-playing records and magazines and books about recording. He does not have a very impressive stereo.

I have come back to my room to go to bed. It is eleven o'clock. I have drunk half a bottle of wine that was left over from last night. I do not feel tired, except when I think about tomorrow. I only have to work in the morning, but Saturday mornings always seem very long.

Day Six

It is ten o'clock and I am contented because I know that he is coming to see me, and tomorrow is Sunday. It is some sort of achievement to have achieved nothing in a day and still feel good about it. It is one of Nature's ironies that Saturday mornings are always fresh and fair. I sat in that spotlit box of ties, scarves, shirts and cashmere, for what seemed like twelve hours but was of course only four. I smoked ten cigarettes. No one came in until it was about time to leave, when a well made-up, thirty-something-year-old woman came in and kept me for an hour. She spent three hundred pounds, buying shirts and choosing ties to go with them, for her family. When, at last, I made out the bill a very hefty uniformed chauffeur entered the shop to check the account before any money changed hands. She, it seemed, was some Eastern princess, and this wrestler her appointed bodyguard. To my untravelled eye she might have come from no further afield than Bromley, but then wealth shows and the rich, however, do look different. When, very occasionally, my friends visit me at the shop, they look unpolished.

I stayed on to clear up the mess and lock away the cash. An hour's unpaid overtime. I was too lazy to be fussed queuing for a bus in Oxford Street. Instead I wandered through Selfridge's, marvelling at how many things I did not want to buy. Then I walked all the way home, buying Elsie's bits and pieces and taking them to her on the way.

Elsie was in a state of excitement: her picture had arrived from the mail order firm. I was actually shocked when I saw it, shocked more by her lack of self-consciousness and my own pre-digested layers of taste; even the taste for bad taste let me down for a while. Right across the width of the chimney breast in her front room, where her husband has his bed, was the long narrow picture. A nude man stood at one edge, gazing towards a nude woman at the other, a surreal landscape behind them, overawed by a mighty swan. I felt as embarrassed as the separated couple, as devoid of words as they were of rude bits. The easy vocabulary, texture, period, even kitsch, were not Elsie's.

I just stuttered, "Amazing," which in a way summed it all up.

Day Seven

Maybe I was too drunk. I do not think so. Or maybe he came and I did not hear him. I woke up sad. I tried to pull myself together. I had a bath which is not a very pleasant experience with a hangover. I retuned the radio to Radio Four just to hear a human voice. I phoned Jane, a long-standing friend, and it is arranged that we meet tomorrow night, if she can find a babysitter. I will phone her from work during the afternoon. I was amazed that it was only ten o'clock in the morning when all this was over. I walked to the Angel and took the tube to Tooting Bec to see my mother. I can always be sure that she is at home at lunchtime on a Sunday. Sure enough she opened the door, all neat, with her pinny on.

"Darling. What a lovely surprise."

We went through to the sitting-room and I slouched on to a chintz-covered sofa.

"Sorry that I didn't phone but I just thought that I would come over and see you."

"Is everything all right?"

"Yes, of course, everything's just fine." I felt myself closing up. I can never think of anything to say to her and I do not like it.

"Are you still working in that shop?"

I know that she hates it that I do what she considers worthless jobs after all the opportunities I have had, like grammar school (grammer skool?), all the things that she never had.

"Yes; it's a bit boring but it's all right. It's very easy."

We sip sweet Cyprus sherry: I feel slightly better.

"I've bought a little chicken and there are peas and potatoes. They're so cheap now, chickens. I remember when you were a child it was a bit of a luxury to eat chicken."

Darling woman, how does she manage to remain polite with a lout like me?

"Are you sure there's enough? I should have phoned. I have masses of food at home."

"Don't be silly. Of course there's enough. Do you want to wash your hands before dinner?"

I dutifully go to the ground-floor lavatory, where there is a hand basin and a neatly folded towel over a rail beside it.

When I came back, the table was laid, and my mother came out of the kitchen with two neat plates of food. We sat opposite each other. There was a glass jug of water on the table.

She said: "There is some wine — I think in the cupboard — if you would like some. I don't drink it."

I refused, genuinely not wanting any. The food tasted delicious. I refused a second helping, but I took a second helping of the pudding: apple pie and custard. Between us we cleared the table and washed up. There seemed to be an amazing amount of things to wash up.

She said: "You leave this. Go and sit down, and

have a rest; you've been working all week."

Finally we both sat down, on the chairs of the chintz-covered three-piece suite, and drank tea. There is a round white plastic trolley always laid ready for tea at my mother's; all she has to do is to boil the water and take the milk out of the fridge. It is the first thing that she does every morning.

I suspect that she wants to watch the film on television but is too polite to turn the set on. We go through the french doors at the back of the room and into the small garden where the spring flowers remain in place, faded like paper facsimiles. There won't be many apples this year, she tells me, looking up into the branches of the overgrown Cox's tree. The trunk is grey from whiting. I like the garden; however much she potters about in it, it always looks as if it's a bit overgrown and neglected. Above the wooden perimeter fence are fixed high trellises to keep out the neighbouring cats. The roses roll and weave their spiny stems above us, each rampage rich in new buds, green and maroon. I feel very dull, unable to respond to this rectangle of trapped nature. We go back inside, and after some desultory news of the family I tell her that I must leave, that I have things to do before tomorrow. "Yes, I'm sure you do," she says, with no edge to the words.

As I stand up to leave, she starts one of her old complaints: "I do wish that you wore skirts; you used to look so nice, and I liked your hair when it was cut short."

Poor Mummy, she must be sad. There we were, just minutes before, looking at the photographs of my cousin Gordon's wedding, and she has this hefty daughter, twenty-seven years old, unmarried, always wearing trousers. I kiss her and leave. Halfway along the tree-lined road I look back.

She is still standing at the gate, one hand in front of her apron, the other raised, waving to me. I love her. I am quite like her, she must know this. The knowledge pleases and displeases me; I have become accustomed to it. I wave and turn the corner. I never have any duty to see Elsie at the weekends because her husband is at home then. And back in my room I really had nothing to do. I lay on the bed. At four o'clock Pasquale came by. He has bought a new car! The old one seemed all right to me, but then I am only a passenger. I knew that he was saving for the new one, that was one of the reasons he worked extra hours in the film laboratory. He whirls me through Dalston, Hackney, the City and home again, not a light against us, the streets ghostly quiet: it is Sunday afternoon. He has to leave to see his uncle again. He gives me a big kiss and a hug and I feel great.

After knocking, I wait at the door of the house next to the one I live in. My landlord's wife opens it. I hand her my week's rent, sorry I did not pay it yesterday. "Would you like to come in for a cup of tea?" she asks me. She is Indian, worked as a child psychiatrist before she married, and now has two children of her own. Her husband is English, of German parents, and works as a chemist in a big teaching hospital. Their kitchen is large, with a glass door leading to steps into the garden. The walls are covered with splashy children's pictures. When her husband Siegfried comes in from the garden we all drink tea from hand-made mugs. I realize that I worry them a bit, not having a career or a fixed man, and they are always subtly trying to figure out the scheme behind my apparently patternless existence. I enjoy telling them that there is nothing beyond what they see and what they know of me: they cannot really accept that. I go back to my room.

All evening I have listened to the radio and read a book about a lonely but well-off woman who has had a baby after a one-night stand. I write a letter to Ms Drabble and another to Ms Lessing. I am always writing to writers, I think they might enjoy hearing from readers; but I never post any of the letters, even the ones I have corrected four or five times. I remain just a digit in their royalty statements.

Since Pasquale had said that he would come and see me, I had thought that he would have come earlier. Now it is half-past ten.

Day Nine

Last night I went to the cinema with Jane. During the day it did not seem possible that I would make it. The previous night Pasquale had paid a visit around midnight, together with two bottles of Barolo, and we did not go to bed until two o'clock. All day yesterday I felt like death but the walk to Oxford Circus woke me up and the film, Jane's choice, was lovely, slow and interesting — an Indian film. Jane is cerebral. She has been through mysticism, politics, drugs and is now being the real thing, so she says, yet again: she is a working unmarried mother. At the end of the show, we walked through Soho and caught the 14 bus to Fulham Road to her flat to relieve the baby sitter. Fortunately baby was asleep so there was nothing to disturb us. I was quite touched that she had prepared a sweet meal for us: potato and water-cress soup, then kippers, which were so good I wonder I do not eat them more often. We discussed the film, which she had seen in terms of the Indian

Mutiny (known as the rebellion in India) and society disintegrating under colonial rule; to me it illustrated the enduring friendship of two men, despite the events of their times. We drank a bottle of pleasant white wine from Sainsbury's. The wine was finished with the meal and I remember thinking how one bottle is no longer enough between two people. I slept on her spare bed, in the living-room, and, having refused a sheet, had a rather prickly night under a duvet but on top of a goatskin.

No sooner had I come in from work tonight than I fell asleep. Now, at ten-thirty, I feel quite awake, drinking a bottle of wine — Italian white, it calls itself — waiting for Pasquale to come, although I am not quite sure why. Pasquale and I probably have nothing to say to each other.

Jane and I shared a flat long ago in Earls Court. Her boy friend (then) was my boy friend's (then) best friend. All three of them had just come down from university, whereas I had just come up from teacher's training college — you cannot get much lower than that. Those were our days of poverty and dreams. The thing that I really miss of those times is the laughter. Young men seemed to me so clever and so amusing. I sound like an old woman.

Day Ten

When he comes tonight I will tell him that it is all over. We can be friends, not lovers.

Last night he accused me of being unfaithful to him. I told him he was boring.

We went to a local wine bar, where he had arranged to meet two of his friends. They were rather flattering to me and the place was unpretentious but gay, in the old sense of the word. The conversation, as far as I can remember it, was about the differences between Italy and England. I had to lean heavily on Pasquale's arm to get to the car and from the car into the room. I remember we started to make love passionately, but I cannot remember how it finished. I suppose I fell asleep. For me alcohol is the most marvellous aphrodisiac, with music and smell tying for second place.

I had not meant to drink tonight, I have only had a couple of glasses.

I know it will hurt, that I will want to go on seeing him. Maybe it will be a sweet experience. A Nigerian student who once lodged upstairs told me that his idea of sexual bliss was to go and go and never come. I can imagine that for ages I will try and glimpse Pasquale as I pass the restaurant. It will always be something like this for it cannot be black and white, wholly wrong or right. But it is wrong enough for me; I want more company; I do not know quite what I want; but it is not this.

Now there is a knock at the door.

Day Eleven

I am so angry with myself.

Last night I went to the door and opened it, staying behind it as I did so. He opened it very slowly, then turned and kissed me. We went into my room and sat on the bed. His face was very close.

"Say it outright: you want to leave me!"

It was shocking, how did he know? He did not. I denied it.

"Alberto likes you. Why don't you go with him?"

"Do you want me to?"

"No, but if you like him, you should go."

"And if I like you, what should I do?" I was laughing, I was actually enjoying these stupidities. Was it because there were so few to follow, it was nearly over, I was letting it last a bit longer? I loved him then, last night.

"Why are you laughing?"

I could not answer, so I put my arm around him to kiss him but he pushed me away, and I remembered then what I had reasoned before, that I had begun to confuse pain with love, strong feelings with reality. With a strong urge to win, slowly slowly I won him round and then it was possible once again to leave him.

Day Twelve

Another day on the edge of my being, chemically cut off by drink and cigarettes. Jeremy came into the shop this afternoon with a bottle of champagne. We drank it from plastic cups donated by the woman in the nearby snack bar. I felt more wholesome after a cup or two. On the way home from work I stopped at the off-licence and bought a bottle of Frascati. At the gate I saw Pasquale waiting for me. He took the paper-covered bottle from me. I had entertained the idea of going over to see Elsie. I thought that the wine was a good Italian one, but he said that it is ordinary plonk if you come from near Rome, as he does. A failure and this bottle was the first of my offerings.

I am backing out of the affair, leaving behind me a trail of tributes for him to trip over. When he left to go to work I was thinking of future gifts. In the wardrobe, under a sweater on the floor of the hanging part, I keep two envelopes, big and beige, a gift from Jeremy. In one I put money for the week: twenty pounds for fares, rent, gas and a long list of small things that are necessary to keep a tidy life ticking along. The other envelope is my secret, my lovely treasure. Each week I add to it and I enjoy writing the amount on the outside and then adding it to the previous total. Last Friday the final total was three hundred pounds, round and real. I had once thought that Pasquale and I might go to Italy on holiday, but nothing ever came of that idea. I want to take him out to dinner. I want to buy him the watch he likes. If I do both of these things I will still have some money left over and maybe we can be over too.

He said he would be round early tonight but it is nearly eleven o'clock and he has not come back. There is very little wine left, but he is bringing his own anyway. I find it hard to believe that the restaurant gives him so much free wine, but maybe it is some sort of tax dodge.

He said that he will come back tonight. He is also going to meet me for lunch, or we might buy some food at Justin de Blank's and have a picnic if the weather is fine. It is as if he knew that I am trying to end it and now he is making a big effort to continue our friendship, to win me round again. Or maybe he is fed up too and trying to cover his guilty tracks. If that is the case it is going to be a dead heat at the finish and this is turning out to be the Glamour Stakes.

I keep seeing his face as it was when he refused my kiss. His full lips pout and his cheeks, usually with some childlike fullness, hang a little. His eyes are dark brown and direct, but I see them as they were then, always avoiding mine. His hair is parted at the side, with locks hanging over one side of his forehead, like an English schoolboy. I think of it as lovely to touch but forbidden at that remembered moment. I am going to enjoy my nostalgic suffering.

I get fed up having time on my hands and not much to do. I would not want to go out every night; but the way I live at the moment, the details are really taking me over. I have just finished cleaning the room and I have tidied the fridge downstairs. While I was working I was thinking about my childhood in South London. I suppose for everyone their own childhood is the most important period to ponder over. The only time I remember when this was not so was in between, in my youth, when childhood was really a thing of the past.

A huge heavy thud against one of the walls of the house made the funiture rattle, as if it was the most natural ordinary thing that demolition work had started — beside my childhood, that was nothing. A bomb explosion is reported on the radio in Italy, killing fifty or more people, and my thoughts shift again to Pasquale, and I want to see him. I want my love.

Day Thirteen

Last night he did not come back.

This morning I woke up to another fine day with the sun not in the usual place, which is halfway along the wall towards the door; it shone a golden pillar on the wardrobe. It is more difficult for me to respond to a beautiful day than to a dull one. I still had two hours before I had to catch the bus to work, but no ideas worthy of such a bright morning. I took a turn around the squares and terraces of Canonbury but the geometry did nothing for me. I returned with two doughnuts and *The Times*, a solid start to the day. Then I lay on the bed in the sunlight and read and ate and sipped coffee.

I phoned the restaurant from work and the manager said that Pasquale had not been in for three days.

After work I went to the small house, off Charlotte Street, his family home. I heard a moan as I went up the rickety wooden stairs after his little sister, fourteen-stone Maria. His mother was at the table, her head in her hands. She is usually well held together, big but elegant; today her overall, or it may have been a dress, looked about two sizes too small for her. As she turned her face towards me I saw all the features thrown somehow into relief, the adjective worn became real. The grandmother, Pasquale's father's mother, was at the sink, her fat legs apart and her head bowed over some task; the father was not there. I sat opposite the mother. Maria sat next to her and put a chubby arm across the woman's shoulders. Her head shaking as if to deny the words, she sniffed and spoke:

"My boy, Pasquale, he's in prison. They put him in prison, I don't understand it, he not a bad boy, you know him. Maybe he was in bad company. I don't know what has happened. The police came, they told us just that he is in prison. His father is so angry, he don't even see his friends, he don't say nothing about it. Please, you go and see Pasquale."

She reached down to the floor, to her large black leather handbag. "Here, take the money for a taxi. Maria no go to a prison, my legs are too bad. Please, help my boy!"

She was handing me a wad of pound notes. I

refused them.

I felt like a missionary on my journey to Brixton but any feeling of grandeur fades within yards of a prison. If I were Queen I would refuse to put my name to such awful-looking places. I joined the queue in the cold shadow of the great side wall, where we hunched up against the chill. Children whimpered and whined and were smacked viciously. Ordinarily I remain unaware that such violence against children still exists. The whines erupt into screams and I begin to feel ill. This is the criminal class, I thought; the pain is passing from one generation to the next.

After twenty minutes, at just two minutes past four o'clock, a small door in one of the massive gates was shoved open. We stepped in to make an untidy file into the corridor at the end of which sat the warder at a high, old-fashioned wooden desk. Everyone had a form to fill in to say who they were and who they were visiting. I had a great disinclination to write my own name down, to be associated in any particular with anything in this grease-covered, chipped gloss-painted, gloomy place. We passed along to a hole in the wall where another warder received any (allowable) gifts for the prisoners. The warder was obviously thinking that everything handed over for inspection must be too good for the people inside — he turned every item over in his hands and muttered: "Players indeed! Chocolate indeed! Books indeed!" None of the things seemed to me worthy of even his dull envy. I left Maria's half-bottle of wine (indeed!) and some sweets and chewing-gum as a present from me; he does not smoke. Still holding a form apiece, we were allowed into the waiting-room. The air was stale with tobacco, the long benches and the walls all scratched, the lino tiles chipped and burned. I sat down until I saw that the slips of paper had to be shoved through a peephole in a door at the far end of the room. When I came back from delivering mine there was no place left to sit down. Some others went up and knocked on the peephole to have it opened and their slips of paper taken in. A little girl of maybe three or four stood on a bench next to the door and tapped on the peephole, which the warder opened. She poked the face of her doll over the opening. The door slammed into the doll's face. I marvelled at the enterprise of children, even in these forbidding surroundings. A woman, her mother almost certainly, grabbed the little girl by her arm and pulled her viciously so that she fell to the floor only to be immediately pulled up by the same arm and receive a walloping slap across the back of her legs. So much for a bit of fun.

With the crashing of several locks, the door opened many times and names were called into the room, so that the visitors went through in ones and twos. Eventually I heard "Rossetti!" and, somewhat dazed, I too walked through the door. There was a lot of noise on the other side. Two high desks with warders at them faced each other between two long rows of Formica tables. Some other warders patrolled up and down between the tables. Prisoners sat on the inside, visitors on the outside, where the chairs, two for each table, could not be put square to the tables because space was so cramped. I was told to sit at a particular table; the chair opposite me was empty. A warder stood and gazed at me. I examined his thick leather belt, the huge ring of keys hanging from it. It is hard not to dislike people girded with this paraphernalia, which remains the unchanged badge of the profession direct from the Middle Ages.

Pasquale approached, with two warders

following him. He turned and glared at them. I thought that he might hit them and I think possibly they might have had the same thought. His face relaxed, nearly to a smile, when he saw me. He sat down opposite me and took my hand into his. We leant across the table and kissed. My head was suddenly full of clichés: "You don't have to tell me if you don't want to....I know it was not really your fault...." But it was his turn to cliché first.

"Listen carefully to what I have to tell you... you're the only person I can trust....Why are you smiling?"

A warder stood right behind him and he lowered his voice further.

"Tell my mother not to worry because I'm all right. Ask my father to do just one thing in his life for me, to get hold of the Italian lawyer — he knows the one I mean."

The warder moved away, Pasquale continued:

"Those things were important — this is more important: you remember the new Fiat, the one you saw the other day. Go to the restaurant and get the keys from my coat that I left there. The car's parked on the corner of Arlington Square. Drive it to the long-stay car park at London Airport. Don't give your real name, for God's sake. Don't tell anyone. Do you understand?"

I nodded. "I don't know where Arlington Square is. . . . Oh, sorry — of course, I can look it up."

"I hate to ask you this, to do this, I mean, but you're the only one. Katie, I love you, I want to live with you. Do you believe me? I hate to ask you, really."

"I'm sure you do. I promise I'll try and do it. Do you want me to bring you anything?"

"Tomorrow I come up to the magistrate. If he doesn't let me go free, bring me some Italian magazines. They have nothing on me."

I did not like him, he was behaving in a self-righteous way, I thought. He was told to leave. We kissed sweetly, the skin of our lips not wanting to separate. I was the one who was left. I sat, the words *I have promised, I have promised* kept going through my mind. The warder on my side of the table told me to leave, Miss.

Day Fourteen

Revelations of a criminal mind. I realize as I write this that it is stupid to put these things on to paper, but my diary has become like a friend, or an attentive analyst; and, besides, who else can I tell?

The restaurant is full to bursting on Sunday lunchtimes. For that very reason I chose to go there at a quarter-past one. The place seemed to be in uproar as the customers — three-generation Italian families — conducted their normal everyday table conversations. I spotted the manager, who was talking to a father seated at the head of a family table. The manager looked a bit annoyed as he saw me approaching, excused himself from his customer and met me halfway down the central aisle. Once it was all smiles when we met; I suppose he is pissed off with Pasquale and so with me, as well.

"I have come from Pasquale's mother to collect the things that he left here. He may be going to Italy."

I hoped that the message would not bring any trouble down on Pasquale. It was the only thing I could think of to say; I do not know who knows what, or even what what is. The manager called

over one of the waiters, who had been one of the
group with whom I had drunk wine about a week or
so ago — it seemed like years. He smiled and said
ciao. The manager told him to bring me anything of
Pasquale's that he could find in the back of the
restaurant. The customers eyed me, and the
manager was whispering something about me to
the father figure whom he had rejoined. Piero came
from the service door with a few garments over his
arm. I took them in both hands and left nearly
banging into the propped-open door on the way
out.

I hurried away, getting nearly halfway along
Essex Road before I stopped, sat on a conviently low
wall and put the things down beside me. No coat,
but a cardigan with pockets, and under a crumpled
tissue in one of the stretched pockets I found a
triangle of plastic with a metal keyring attached to
it and two keys, one small and one large. I held the
tissue to my nose and then wiped my wet forehead,
I put it back into the pocket. In the other pocket I
found a folded pound note. Apart from the cardigan
there were two T-shirts, both white, neither clean
nor very dirty. I held them to my nose. They
smelled human and friendly. I rubbed them against
my cheeks.

It was hot all the way to Arlington Square and I
resented having to carry the things. *Maybe the police
are following me*, I thought. Quite likely; it is probably
all a trap and the manager is in on it, which makes
that friendly smile on Piero's face ghastly, if he
knows too. Now they will wait to see what I do next
before stopping me. I could not see anyone
following me. The carefully laid out council estate
gave way to gentrified terraces and the squares of
lower Islington. Well, I suppose so, if I remembered
the map correctly. The map was in my bag but I did

not have to look at it — I was already in Arlington Square.

There was the car, at the corner of the inside kerb. Leaves from the garden in the centre of the square had fallen on the car and there was a general powdering of dust over the shine. I gazed round furtively, before putting my bag and Pasquale's things on the bonnet of the car. The key would not make the door open. It had to be the small one but nothing happened, even when it turned. I was sweating; was this Pasquale plotting against me now? Every day I see motorists opening cars — it cannot be that difficult. Finally when it worked, it was so easy but there seemed no reason why. Inside the car was like an oven. I needed to cool and collect myself but my heart was thudding out the message that with five or six driving lessons in my life (and they happened about a year ago with an old boy friend), if it was not anyway so illegal, it would still be illegal for me to drive — apart from moral considerations.

The Fiat started straight away then immediately stalled. This happened three times before I jerked forward in first, finding it some comfort that the numbers of the gears were on the top of the stick. Jerking and stalling a couple of times more, I got the hand brake off and the car leapt forward, just missing a passing taxi. Thank goodness there was no need to reverse, the street ahead of the square left enough room for a left turn before forming a T-junction with City Road. One right turn and then, with growing confidence, I went into second. A steady twenty miles an hour seemed dangerously fast, but anything less and the car would look suspiciously slow. I felt safe, after a while, in second. At the lights by Gray's Inn Road I stalled, or rather the car stalled, and we only got off just as they were changing again, little leaps and bounds. The driver of the car that I had left behind must have been able to divine that there was not a competent person at the wheel. Very few cars along Charing Cross Road, the Mall, past Harrods; I knew the route as if I had driven it every day of my life. After Cromwell Road I was touching thirty but still by far the slowest thing on the road. *They are all criminals*, I chuckled to myself.

I turned the key and the engine stopped. I felt lightweight and the air tasted good. I went to the office hut. I said I was off to the USA for a few months, my voice high-pitched and rather shaky, as I gave a name of a girl who used to live at the same address, when the house was full of middle-class white people like me (now I am the only white person left, the others have all moved on). The girl whose name I used works for the *Daily Telegraph*. The man looked at me for what seemed like a second too long and I wondered whether he knew the girl. He told me to park in a certain bay, to bring the keys back and that there would be a bus along in a few minutes. I felt bad waiting with so few other people. I stood near someone else's luggage and then boarded the bus. I had begun to enjoy the ride but I got out at the first stop, which turned out to be the terminal for international flights.

Packaged pilgrims like ants crawled all over, up and down the modern interior. I had about eighty pounds sterling in my bag and I wondered if I would not be wise to buy a ticket and leave the country, but I did not have my passport. My bag bulged with Pasquale's things folded into it. I felt like a stupid holidaymaker. I treated myself to a cup of coffee and a bun, nothing else was tempting. I started to smoke a cigarette, giving up on the bun halfway. I had no appetite because I had not eaten all day. I went to catch the bus to Victoria, but my newly-found criminal awareness stopped me. I went instead to the tube.

By the time I had reached the Angel, I was sick of public transport and I walked the rest of the way back. A warm, sullen Sunday in the city.

Back in my room, no music that I could find on the wavelengths suited my mood. I could not lie still, nor find any activity to match the activity in my mind. I went upstairs to find the Nigerian student of dental hygiene. We had had a longish conversation in the kitchen about a week ago and I had come away nearly convinced that dental hygiene was the key to our future happiness. Her room is lined with cardboard boxes, which also serve as furniture, each one topped with a lacy cloth and then an item of consumer durability. All these boxes are to be filled and taken to Lagos with her when her course is finished. On one case sits a big black and white television. We drank beer from cans and watched robot people outwitting baddies. For the first hour all the action seemed lovely — it converted my own sublimated energy — but then grew unbearably tedious. I found I could not stop an ever more rapidly recurring sequence of stretches, yawns and fidgets. After refusing a cup of nourishing Horlicks ("We all drink it in Nigeria, and you know it's good for you") I left.

Although it is only nine o'clock I am in to a hastily bought bottle of plonk and my diary. Time is moving slowly, or has it speeded up?

In a way I am, I suppose, quite pleased with myself. But I do not admire Pasquale any the more for what I have had to do and what he has been up to. It's not like the old-time films where the detectives, with a mixture of luck and hard work, came up with the facts. In a way I suppose it must be a little sad for the criminals to be dealing with slow-witted cops.

Now I half-expect a knock at the door.

Tomorrow Pasquale will come up before the magistrates. I will ring the prison from work to see if he is in or out. I have put the car-park ticket at the back of the wardrobe under a gym shoe.

Now you know it all.

Funny, that he will not call.

Day Ifteen

The heading, a true slip. A chirpy day. I locked up shop at one o'clock and made my way through Mayfair to the fine Dickensian-sounding firm of Messrs Gabbitas–Thring, Educational Consult-ants, Sackville Street. Having provided a heavily expurgated version of the curriculum vitae I was given a comforting interview by a matronly woman who said that notice of any suitable posts would be sent to me through the post. I was back in the shop at two o'clock and that was after having a celebratory coffee and soggy sardine sandwich as well. No one noticed my absence, it seemed.

After all the nights of longing to see him, now that I have him literally captive I am torturing him. I did not go down to Brixton to tell him the news. It costs money, I told myself — it must be hard for poor families, that is true — I wanted to come home (God knows what for, just because it is here).

Very unpredictable stuff, alcohol; sober one night and drunk the next.

Life seems to have a pattern for other people, or so it would seem to an outsider. Most people (big generalization, of course) find a job, a career and get married for better or for worse, but there is some discernible pattern. (Rubbish, self-centred rubbish. I, too, have a category, big-city lonely, millions of us.)

I never wanted to marry; I never wanted to be lonely; I never wanted to be a gay socialite. I cannot think of what I never wanted to be, let alone what I might want to be. Elusive stuff, life. My feeling is that I am seizing up on wine and cigarettes; the details are taking over again.

Day Sixteen

His face, his whole body, just seemed to relax when I whispered to him that I had done what he asked me to do. He took my hands and kissed them, and everything was fine for a few minutes, but after them there did not seem to be anything to say. I would have been just satisfied to sit and gaze at him but there was some sort of pressure at work on us that we had to use the short time we had together.

He said in a deliberate raised voice, "They only kept me inside because I'm a bloody foreigner."

I felt like saying: "You're a bloody thief." But, of course, I could not. I do wish that he could tell me what he has been up to, I deserve to know. He has to wait for another four days of Her Majesty's pleasure and my displeasure, before he sees the magistrates again.

It seemed quite late by the time I got back. I timed my eating to have some music to accompany me. The timing was all right; I had finished eating and had lit a cigarette as Georg Solti and the Chicago Symphony Orchestra slid into the slow movement of Mahler's Fifth, and I into my fifth glass of wine.

It is ten and no one is going to come and see me. I am bored with my job and lonely and not even drunk. I might as well go to bed.

When I look around this room I realize that I know what is in every drawer, in every envelope, it is all me. How can it be any other way?

Day Seventeen

Jeremy came in at eleven o'clock this morning and I told him that I had to have an hour off at lunchtime. He looked quite sick and asked me to leave it until tomorrow. He was sorry to ask me — of course I could have a lunch break, but he had arranged to have lunch not just with the editor of *Vogue* but together with Bianca and four other fashionable people. I said that I had things that also had to be done today. Finally it was arranged that I take some time off during the afternoon. At quarter to four he came back from lunch and I left.

I collected a plastic bag of things after waiting ages for Pasquale's grandmother to come down to the door. His mother and sister sew all day in a clothes workshop (his father has some illness which prevents him working but not from going to the betting shop and drinking club). Then I hurried to Soho and bought a pile of Italian magazines and some Italian cigarettes — he must have been driven to smoking, poor old thing, or maybe he trades them for something or other.

The only picture I retain in my mind of the scene beyond the interview area is of three men in a cell not wanting to listen or talk to each other; they play Radio One on a transistor radio night and day. Not quite true: at night they listen to Capital Radio.

I was back in the shop at five o'clock, the place in a great mess, there had been a rush, Jeremy looking very flustered. For no good reason, I felt like a naughty truant but quite pleased about it. He left to see someone important and I cleared up. He came back just as I was locking up, to collect the money, then left me to finish locking the door. As he was on his way out I asked if he could give me a lift to Brixton Prison. Alas, he did not know where Brixton was.

A rather strained visit, with Pasquale again murmuring his thanks and his love and his promises of a better future.

Since coming back, I have unpacked a huge bag of food I bought in the Greek shop in Essex Road. I bought it with the thought that eating was a common and reliable anodyne for loneliness. None of the stuff seems at all appetizing. I unpacked it into the cupboard and fridge downstairs. I ended up eating the cheese sandwich which had sat in my bag all day. Now I drink from a half-bottle of retsina that I had intended as an accompaniment to the tinned stuffed vine leaves and *pitta* bread, for which I paid a small fortune to the unshaven Petros (who holds my hand when I pay him).

It is half-past ten, a knock at the door, but this is the inside door.

Day Eighteen

Eleven o'clock and I have only just come in. I had told Pasquale that I would not go and see him today. During the day I began to feel bad about him, stuck inside without even one visitor. So I went.

He asked me if it were true that the English are

either educated and marvellous or else they are sluttish, unstylish oafs. I defended the British working class, which involved us in quite a lively chat and we were surprised when the visiting session was over, after what seemed such a short time. I got off the bus at the Angel, went to the pub, I bought myself a half a pint of bitter and sat down. Apart from the staff, I knew no one. At nine-ish I went out, bought a bag of chips and ate them walking around the balmy backwaters of Chapel Street. I looked up at Janet's window but there was no light. She has a bare room above a shop in Chapel Street. During the days she sells vegetables from a stall. I first met her when I worked in the pub. She likes to drink, she has lots of friends but is a quiet middle-aged woman — maybe half a man, if you believe the tales or the grey blue of her chin sometimes. When I went back to the pub she was there with a group of locals. When they asked me how my Italian lover was getting on I was not going to tell them the real news but chatted on about the government, Islington and the people we knew in common.

At ten-thirty I left, feeling quite high. I felt like continuing the evening somehow but there was nothing left to follow, except to walk home and hope that the stimulation would wear off.

Last night my neighbour the engineer called to offer me a can of beer. We drank several, sitting in my room. I did not try to find any music on the radio and had no expectation that he would share my taste in cassettes. It was neither awkward nor was it a social triumph. Soon I must go to the laundrette, face the Greek women's branch of the Mafia. Sophoclean heroines can be readily understood and recognized if you visit Essex Road Laundramatic. The women, mainly clad in black, brandish bleached sticks with which they prod the clothes. These same sticks also serve to keep others away from the dryers until they are satisfied that none of the clan has any further requirement for one. Here the play unfolds, at a mechanized river bank, where a week's washing for a humble British subject can take up to three hours. I am down to scrabbling about the bottom of my laundry bag until, like an archaeologist, I come upon an epoch when clothes were deposited to be washed in a far less soiled state than is the case nowadays.

Friday tomorrow: the thought lifts my spirits, although I have promised that I will go to work this Saturday.

Day Nineteen

As I came in this evening the telephone was ringing. My mother wanted to hear that I was still in the land of the living, as she put it. I told her I had seen Jane and that Jane had a lovely baby boy, forgetting that she did not know that Jane had already divorced her husband, who my mother knew because years ago, before he married Jane, he was a boyfriend of mine. My mother was left with the false impression of a solid nuclear family. I felt rather bad about the deceit and will put it right some time in the future. She spoke fondly of the couple but I remembered how she had disliked Edward when she thought that I might marry him. Now I suppose her standards have lowered, having an ageing spinster daughter "on the shelf". She bravely claims that (maybe) I am wise never to have married, that the way the world is going it is better not to bring any children into it, but I know, and my aunts hint at it, how she would love nothing more than to have a baby in the family again. I told her that I cannot go and see her this weekend, but not why; I say that I will phone her next week; with the customary endings of "Do you need anything? . . . Don't work too hard. . . . Take care of yourself. . . . Are you sure that you're all right? . . ." by which time she has heard the annoyance in my voice so it is: "Goodbye, darling." Then I say "Thank you for ringing, goodbye, goodbye," all in a jolly tone, and it is over.

When I came downstairs and unlocked my door I found a buff envelope on the lino. I found that I was frightened to open it. I put it on the table and went downstairs to make a pot of tea. Back in my room, armed with a cuppa and a cigarette, I felt strong enough to tear the beastly thing open.

Inside the envelope were two economy-sized slips of paper, both headed Gabbitas–Thring. One offered a position as a mistress in an independent girls' school in Hertfordshire, general arts subjects with one period of games a week, the successful applicant expected to live in. The other was headed *Governess with one ten-year-old boy, Kensington area*, "salary and terms by arrangement" typed underneath. There was a telephone number. That one I will ring tomorrow. No more schools for me, if I can help it, although an independent girls' school in Hertfordshire would certainly be less pee-and-milk-smelling than an ILEA primary, and there would be no need for forty screaming children imprisoned in the same room all week with only me and a few battered books as an outlook on to the world. But would the staff-room be less desultory? I doubted it and poured myself another cup of tea.

All day today it has been grey and raining. In the shop I felt quite cosy and insulated until it became stuffy — sometime around midday — and I had to go out for a brisk walk. I found it just as muggy as inside so I took a cup of coffee back to work with me. I spent my time reading *The Times* and the *New Statesman*, because I do not have a book to read. I was going to the launderette but the weather is against it. Instead I ate fried bacon and egg and listened to a programme about a trial in the thirties of a medium who sued a newspaper for libel, the verdict inconclusive. I did the washing up, chatted to the dental hygiene student while she prepared her daily dish of ground rice pounded to a starchy mass with another panful of chicken floating in red gravy — I call it red death because it is ninety per cent chilli powder, something I never want to eat again in my life.

I accepted an invitation to take Horlicks with Mrs Dental Hygiene and we went upstairs to her room. The television was on. She ate while I watched and sipped the sickly stuff, which I quite like, really; it was like a dessert. Then I discovered a pile of magazines, on a shelf under her coffee table. I took them out one after the other, *Playboys* and *Penthouses*, all about a year out of date. She giggled when she saw them in my hand.

"My husband bought them when he was over last year."

I could not stop reading on and on, especially captivated by the readers' letters to *Penthouse*. Every letter warmed up with a statement that the writer was an avid reader of the magazine and then went on, because it might be of interest to other readers, to describe a personal sexual adventure. All the cocks enormous (and many circumcised) in the land of swimming-pools, apartments softly furnished, the fantasies and their realizations all lubricated with come (sperm): an amusement arcade of clits and slits, love sticks and love tunnels, bulges and bosoms. When I had finished my Horlicks I asked to borrow one copy. I took it to my room. Turning the pages in a frenzy of reading, I lay on my bed and masturbated. When it was all over, out of some sort of prudery I put the magazine out of sight in the wardrobe.

I have become an avid reader of pornography just tonight. Now it is eleven o'clock and I will go to my solitary bed. Outside the rain is splashing down. As *Penthouse* would have it, coming down hard.

Day Twenty

I phoned the number for the governess job from work this morning but got no reply. I spent a good half of the morning standing outside the shop in the sunshine, only going inside to smoke. I find it a waste of a cigarette to smoke in the open air, or, in another sense, a waste of the fresh air. A couple of shirts sold, ones that were in the window. Things in the window always get sold easily. The customers usually lack the imagination to look at the rest of the stock to see what combined with what would look very good. I could not be bothered to make a new window display. I took out the remaining stock and put a Chinese umbrella, opened, on the floor of the window. I readjusted the lights and admired the enigmatic look of the piece.

At ten minutes to one I locked up shop, not wanting to be caught out by a late buyer again. I had thought of walking to Brixton but I only got as far as Victoria before I took the tube. It was too early for visiting so I wandered around the market. I recalled how exciting this place had been to me as a child. It still seemed impressive: the great jumbly mass of people and goods, dwarfed nevertheless, first by the railroad and then, at the back, the lesser warrens covered by the great roofs and galleries. I bought some chocolate for Pasquale.

Pasquale has convinced himself that with the lawyers help he will be released next week. "There is nothing against me," he says confidently.

"Good," say I.

He asks me if I have found a new lover.

"Hundreds," I reply and he drops my hands and looks away from me. I take one of his hands and tell him that I have been quite lonely without him. Then he wonders if this is true. . . . I feel a touch of nausea at all this sentimental hogwash. I would gladly change the subject but cannot think of anything to say.

At last time is up; he is led away and I am allowed out of prison. It seems like a mile to walk before the sun touches the earth again.

I could not face the underground and took a bus that had Oxford Street as one of its destinations. The upstairs was almost full, bouncing and babbling with South London children, each with a rolled towel, off to swim. They all got off at Clapham. From somewhere near Tottenham Court Road I walked down towards Covent Garden, hoping to see a friend of mine (who has set up home with a man after a long period as a lesbian). I could not tell if the bell was working but if it was, there was no one at home. I went across the road to the Swan and a half of bitter. When I left, the streets were full of expectant bustle. Such newly washed faces that I could smell the soap and the scents as these decently dressed folk passed me on their ways to the theatres and restaurants of the West End. Outside the Coliseum a man was offering a single seat in the stalls, which I took at something less than the price printed on it.

I felt shop-soiled in my jeans and two-day-old clothes. In the next seat a woman wearing a long dress and fur stole raised her chin level as I sat down, but the elegance was not general. The overture was already a favourite of mine but I had never heard the rest of *The Magic Flute*.

I bought the ticket confident that if I did not like what followed I could just leave, for I feel that I am rich enough to justify such whims. I stayed willingly to the end and we clapped ourselves out with thanks and I would have been happy for the curtain to rise for the whole thing to start again. It was better, I thought, than the best of any Gilbert and Sullivan I had seen, without for a moment conveying to me any of the deeper meaning of significance proposed in the programme notes.

Now it is nearly midnight. I am eating shortbread biscuits and sipping wine. I once lived solely on shortbread biscuits for two whole weeks.

Day Twenty-One

It is only just ten. I have to remind myself that there is no reason to doubt — he will not come.

Whistling Pappageno's song, from *The Magic Flute*, I boarded a bus to Epping Forest and wandered about a bit on the boring earth, feeling sorry for the trees, that they were stuck there; it all seemed so forlorn. In a layby there was a tea van, where the woman attendant told me there is a rapist in the woods. I wonder what Mozart could make of all this. Islington, and even the laundrette are natural and pleasant places after my morning safari. I bought a *Sunday Times* and as usual regretted the purchase, it takes so long to look through, that it shortens the day to no seeming purpose. There was one story, however, that I liked. It was an account of a young woman who wrote a best-selling batch of stories but decided not to write any more because her back ached when she sat for long at the typewriter. Pettiness is an admirable thing: if we were all more petty then the world could be a better place, full of beautifully turned-out philosophers.

I have the complete kit of clean clothes selected and slung over the chair for tomorrow morning. I phoned the number for the job today. A nicely upper-class woman's voice asked me round for tomorrow evening.

I am seriously perplexed whether to finish this bottle of wine, so that I will be nice and drunk, or leave the half that is sitting here now, which has the advantage that I will have it here for tomorrow and also that I will feel better in the morning. If it is a matter of taking or not taking heed of the morrow, the lilies of the field never had to worry about a drink or so too many, or too few.

Day Twenty-Two

Midnight. Today I went for the interview for the job in Kensington.

It was a flat quite near South Kensington underground station. The room we went into, the posh-voiced woman and I, was off a door-lined corridor. It was big and beautiful without being heavy. There were lots of jolly treasures scattered about the white walls and on pieces of polished mahogany furniture. The carpet was light beige in colour, with Persian rugs here and there. I nestled at the edge of a big pale blue feathery sofa and soon had a large tumbler of whisky in my hands. She curled her feet up under her, filling the seat, but not half of the high back, of a winged armchair. There was something shell-like about her; the colours were pale, a pink cashmere sweater, blonde hair, gold and diamond rings on one hand, a grey skirt. She has a fine face: the cheek-bones just visible; a nose with interesting little angles at the nostrils; a near-perfect mouth, not too full; hips and legs a little thick, making her feet look small and neat.

I told her, of course, something of my previous teaching experience. "How horrid for you," she said, when I described my last school job. She told me the boy was ten years old — her husband's, from a previous marriage. There had been a very nasty divorce case. Now her husband had won custody but the boy is very nervous and has been refused a place at the prep school where he had previously been accepted. She asked me some questions: did I speak French? "I used to." (A white one, that.) She told me that she herself spoke fluent French, and could help him. The only surprising question was: did I approve of corporal punishment? I replied, "No," without hestitation, because I find it degrading for both parties. She said that was good, because they had found out that the boy's last tutor was hitting him.

During this part of the conversation I was remembering a letter about a beloved beating from *Penthouse*. Pornography is terribly haunting, like cheap music to Noel Coward. After about an hour of talk she left the room, returning with a well-built pale boy in hand. He loosened his grasp of her hand, allowed his knees to bend further and further until he sank to all fours, then crawled away to a cane rocking-chair at the far end of the room. He curled up in the chair, his knees up to his chest half tight with one arm, the other bent up to thrust a thumb vigourously in and out of his mouth. Rocking, rocking in the chair he watched me from under a mop of soft but spiky fair hair, that was obviously meant to sit in totally other directions. I thought that it showed animal kindness not to look him in the eyes, so I carefully avoided his gaze. I was now sipping at a second well-loaded tumbler and had begun to comprehend that the whole thing was quite interesting, even worthwhile. Soon afterwards we agreed that I could start next Monday. My face felt flushed. I said goodbye to the boy Nicholas first, rock, rock from him. Then I shook hands and said thank you to the woman — Mrs Philips. She calls me Miss Brown; we are going to remain formal, it seems. I suppose I am one of the servants now.

Outside her apartment the cosmopolitan crowd in the West London street seemed better heeled than the Islington lot. I found my bearings and, like most parts of the city, to a Londoner it held associations. I have a girl friend who has lived in a mews flat off the Cromwell Road for as long as I have known her; we met ten years ago when we were both holiday-jobbing in a restaurant.

She opened a narrow door and led me up the steep stairs. I heard voices speaking Italian. "It's my Berlitz cassette," she explained, as we entered the high room carpeted in beige cord with oddments of Victorian furniture.

This place of hers I used to think was dreamy elegant, but it has never changed and now I find it a bit sad. I needed to talk a bit. I had forgotten that she seldom listens and she shortly launched into an abusive tirade against the V and A, where she now works. At first I found the monologue, with its rounded-mouth delivery, mesmerizing. When I grew restless she said that she had nothing to drink in the flat — was this mind-reading?

"I can go out to the local and buy some plonk; but, honestly, it's awful, and terribly expensive."

I agreed to some coffee and it turned out to be very good, lots of it in large cups like those in French cafés. I waited for a decent amount of time to pass before I could get out the magic words, about a train to catch.

I have hardly thought about Pasquale all day. He said that I would forget about him.

Day Twenty-Three

It seems to be my correct dose: a packet of cigs and a bottle of wine to be taken every day.

This evening I went to see him; tomorrow he comes up again. The way he explains it, it really does seem as if they are only keeping him inside because he is foreign. I suppose foreigners are more likely to skip the country. We are all supposed to be equal under the law. To be fair, anyway, things have to be uneven.

I told Jeremy that I am leaving soon. He whimpered on about my finding someone else and quickly made sure that I will work next Saturday morning. I promised that I will help him out on Saturdays, even when I am not working during the week. Even as I said it, I sensed my future resentment. I am developing some imagination at last, so I may even end up with a hobby, apart from this diary-writing.

As I sat in Jenny's flat I glanced at her language

course, cassettes and a booklet. I would like to learn Italian; those foreign words seem so direct, simpler, untainted. Often I use a word and then wonder what I really mean by it, or what other people think it means. I used the word "emotion" while talking to Pasquale this evening, then on the way home started to think out what I meant with it; it would take pages of my diary to sort it out or, rather, to put down the confusion that it means for me.

Day Twenty-Four

He was freed yesterday. He was waiting outside when I came back. Instead of taking me in his arms the moment we got inside, he sat silently looking down at his feet. Maybe he suffers from post-prison depression.

We took a bus to the West End. I led the way to a smart, newish Italian restaurant in Romilly Street, Soho. The food was good. Pasquale had tagliatelli with mushroom sauce; I had ham and melon. He ate some tripe, which I have never tried and so I do not know if I like it or not. I ate liver with butter and sage. We shared a salad and a bottle of Orvieto, and then another half to keep us going. I was afraid that he might find fault (usually the waiters come from the wrong part of Italy), but the service was excellent. Pasquale could have been an English gentleman, for all it showed. We had espresso coffees and brandies and then I paid the bill, producing the money for him to hand over, to save his pretty face. Although it was quite expensive it would have been good value if we had not been so silent, a silence not surprising, since we could hardly talk about the important matter besides which everything else seemed hardly worth mentioning. Along the Charing Cross Road I felt so jolly and the world seemed exciting and sparkling. Losing any reason, I hailed a taxi to take us home.

Back in my room we went straight to bed. A combination of booze and *Penthouse* fantasies made easy pleasure of those acts I almost feared to perform again. They had become absurd considered in the abstract.

Tonight I went to a house off the City Road where he is lodging, because his father will not have him at home. It is the house of some architect friends of his, one of them Italian, one Swiss, the third English. The Englishman, who is away at present working in Australia, had taken the front room on the first floor of this Georgian cottage, then heavily disguised it as something from some future — when future was still an idea.

Half the floor is raised two feet and the whole floor covered with plastic, bright yellow. Two windows and the wall behind the platform are covered in silvery metallic fabric curtains. The ceiling is a mass of bolted-together angle metal, combining television on a runner, a cassette player, speakers, innumerable spotlights and a panel of illuminated square buttons to control the whole mad Meccano reverie. There is a mattress on the platform. We sat on this bed, drinking red wine and eating chicken and chips from a local take-away. Polystyrene plates seemed exactly right.

We made love, then listened to some music from above until the argument started. He would not tell me anything about the car business. He said it was all to do with a friend of his and he became angry when I did not believe him. Then I started to get mad — I had tried to tell him that I had found a new job but he did not bother to listen — so I told him that I had missed a period (it was a lie and I despised myself as I said it). But even this did not interest him, he just said:

"So you must be pregnant. Whose baby is it?"

"Yours, you fool."

"We'll see. . ." he said and then he went on about his family, how he would have to look for a job, how unfair British justice is.

I threw my glass across the room, followed by a jar of pencils that were standing on the platform. They all hit the wall.

"Pick them up!" he commanded. (I would never pick them up.) "What's the matter with you?"

"You don't listen. You don't understand. These things are important." I had my head on my knees and my hands over my head. I should have been crying. He was lying stretched full-length on the bed. I got up, dressed and left.

Now, as I set this event out in words, I feel quite calm. Throwing the things at the wall was a flash of madness that illuminated my little world. The light seemed to change as I threw the stuff. The outburst brought some relief to a tension only perceived in retrospect, when it was suddenly reduced.

Day Twenty-Five

I needed sleep as soon as I came home.

Pasquale came round last night at four in the morning. I was deeply asleep. I could not rouse myself more than to say: "We must be friends, not lovers any more." He wanted to ask questions, to discuss things, but I felt as if I were ill. I lay in bed, covers drawn up to my neck, and I could only repeat the "friends, not lovers" bit. Finally he apologized for coming so late. He came to the bed and sat on it, leaning forward so that his face was close to mine. His eyes were wide, a look of charming innocence.

"Can I ask you one big favour, big, big, big? I know I have asked you favours before and you have always been a good friend to me but this one is big, big, big."

I had to smile at his lovely face.

"Yes, well. Maybe. Probably. What is it?"

"Can we try one more time. I know that I am difficult, but you are difficult as well. One more try?" His head tilted to one side.

I shook mine. "No."

He left. Straight away I was asleep again.

When I woke up, this evening, I ate sardines for my supper and then walked around the streets for a while. I like looking into the windows of people's homes, which is very easy to do if they live in basements. All those pieces of furniture, the floors, the windows, pots, pans, ornaments, and the owners who move it all round and about, moving the dirt a little way off, a constant activity of nest building and maintenance. It reminds me of my mother, for whom most museums are a nightmare of dust traps. She lives in the hope that she will die with all her things in good order and quite clean. She is neat and ready night and day for the great call. Along with half the women of England she could have "RIP. She won't be cleaning any more," engraved on her memorial.

I returned from my walk to find Pasquale at the door, a bottle of champagne in his hand. I consented to share it with him. Then we made love. He has gone back to his future room now, I suppose.

I asked him not to come tomorrow, telling him that I need some independence, even some solitude. He sweetly agreed. We kissed farewell.

I feel like a free woman.

Day Twenty-Six

All week at work I have tidied up and cleaned more than usual. I feel a bit bad, not to be working all the time, now that I am leaving. Today is my last full day. The time passed quite reasonably and I felt a little sad to be leaving my familiar and comfortable post. Jeremy has promised to take me out to dinner next week. I said I would phone him during the week. Tomorrow when I lock up I shall put the key through the letter-box.

Tonight, after supper, I sat down and tried to recall some of the more successful projects from my teaching days. I wonder why the Philips' took me on so readily; maybe a reticence in my manner reassured Mrs Philips. It is going to be nice to have a job where appearances count for much less than at the shop. I will consult the landlord's wife tomorrow; her name is Tahera.

I suppose we are all known by our labels — she is the landlord's wife (to me). I am the girl who works in the shop (to Jeremy), still a stripper to the pub crowd, I suppose. Goodness knows what I am to the other lodgers and the landlord. Maybe I drink so much wine nowadays because I have developed a distaste for it. I cannot bear to finish an evening without the stale taste of cigarettes and wine in my mouth. It is not just the words and names, there are certain realities in all this confusion.

Day Twenty-Seven

I have spent the whole day and an evening alone. A while ago the music turned sad and I felt like crying from stinking self-pity. I am lonely yet I do not seek company. The message is the same for all of us — help. I have sat around enough to become what is called a vegetable, sleeping, reading or listening to the radio. I know that if I move, go out, walk, dance, talk, any of these things, I would feel better. Instead I choose to sit and smoke cigarettes and curse my fate, kidding myself that such dull times will motivate me, thrust me along towards achievement. Probably you cannot just get up out of a chair and achieve — it takes some practice. Motivation can be a tiny thing, like the other day I only went out and found a new job because I felt sick and bored. I might just as well have gone to a pub for a soda water. Results are out of all proportion to the action — usually almost invisible.

Day Twenty-Eight
(written on Day Twenty-Nine)

I woke early, but stayed in bed until the door was banged hard at nine o'clock. It was Pasquale with a bag of still-warm croissants. I made coffee and we ate as though starving, putting crumbs all over the bed. I tried to make conversation. Pasquale looked at me and hardly spoke.

After we had made love we slept on top of the bed, covered by warm sunshine that filled half the room because I had only opened one of the curtains. I woke and looked at him sleeping, taking small panting breaths like a puppy. I kissed him and we rolled together, kissing and hugging, and made love again. After another sleep, Pasquale demanded some lunch. I left the house like a sleep walker, wearing just a T-shirt, cotton skirt and plimsolls. I bought tomatoes, potatoes and eggs. We ate chips, fried eggs, tomato salad with onions in it. Everything tasted delicious. As I cleared the plates I walked behind him and kissed the top of his head, he leant back and kissed me on the mouth. I left the plates on the table and we went back to bed.

When we finally woke it was dark. We took it in turns in the bathroom then, all warm calm and glowing, we walked to an Indian restaurant in the Balls Pond Road and ate satisfying platefuls of spicy rice. Pasquale said that if we did not row life would be paradise. We made a joke of saying "please, not again" every now and then, meaning love-making. I felt such love for him that the expression "making love" seemed just right for us. We walked back to the house, walked around the streets for a moment's digestion before taking a pint of beer each at the dreary local, then back to bed to sleep close together, one or other of us stirring to stroke or kiss the other gently, during the reassuring rest.

Day Twenty-Nine

I woke with a shock at seven o'clock and immediately got out of bed. Pasquale was gone and I had not heard him leave. I was dressed, breakfasted and out at seven-thirty because I did not know how long the journey to Kensington would take. As I left, the cat was crying at the door, so I kicked him to remind him not to go into the house. I was at South Kensington much too early. I went into a café next to the station and had a coffee, which I did not really want, smoked a cigarette and read *The Times* until the time was right to leave.

Nicholas was sitting waiting at the table in the big room when his stepmother showed me in. He turned to grin nervously at me. As I entered she said that she would be out for most of the morning. We heard her leave a few minutes later. On the table were some of the books from his time at school. I looked through them and asked him about them. He showed me his exercise books, typically much neater on the first page than any of the following ones. At the end of the marked exercises were pages full of scribbles and nonsense. His own conception of work? He laughed at these and turned his gaze away from me. I decided to have nothing to do with these previous exercise books and we started off in a new one that was on the table. Together we went through a passage of English comprehension. He did not seem particularly dim, nor did he seem brilliant. Then I asked him to do four of the sums that had been set in his arithmetic book, well before the point at which he had stopped. I left him at the table and took some of the books to a nearby armchair.

I was reminiscing about yesterday until I became aware of a gentle plopping sound. I walked over behind the bent figure of the boy and saw that huge tears were falling on to the clean open page — plop, plop, plop, plop. I sat down beside him, he remained motionless.

"What's all this about — a few silly sums?"

"I can't do them." His voice was choked and dull.

"Well, we can work out how to do them. You won't find it too difficult, I promise." I told him about how as a child I had been frightened to go to school because I could not do my times tables.

He looked at me with wide eyes, but then his head went down again and another plop sounded. "I am sad, I have never been happy."

I just put my hand on his shoulder and gave him a very gentle hug. His misery seemed so logical and so adult that I could not discuss it.

"Come on, let's write a story. We'll make a book with lots of pictures in it."

He sniffed and turned to go and fetch a handkerchief. I cleared the table, opened another new exercise book and put out a set of coloured pencils. I began to wonder if he was coming back and what I would do if he did not. Finally he returned and started his story. We were still deep into the tale when his stepmother came in, accompanied by a man scarcely taller than her but older, about forty, with a suspicion of a paunch, wearing smart city tweeds. This was Nicholas's father. They smiled at us working away at the table.

I stood up to shake hands with Mr Philips. He had a gentle voice through wide lips, his whole face a bit moon-like. He suggested that we should all go out to lunch. Nicholas was giggling, with his head lowered, and he looked rather stupid. He was taken in hand by his parents, one on each side, and he played at not walking by himself, again he was the idiot child. I picked up my cardigan and followed.

We walked to a Chianti-strewn Italian restaurant next to the café where I had had coffee earlier in the day. We all ate *lasagne* and drank red wine, Coca-Cola for Nicholas. It was a sort of celebration so we had puddings, after which I smoked a cigarette with the coffee. Nicholas was asked if he liked his new teacher, he turned away from the questioner, his father, and giggled loudly. We were all quite

satisfied with this answer. Mr Philips remarked —
quite unnecessarily, I thought — that he had
expected a governess to be gaunt, middle-aged and
off-putting. "Soon," I replied, a bit confused. I am
not in good practice for lunchtime drinking and
anyway I was nervous to create a good impression.
It was only good fortune that I hit upon a
reasonably lighthearted reply.

This afternoon we used a big pile of unwanted
Vogue magazines, tearing up suitably coloured
pictures to make a big impressive collage — a jungle
scene. Nicholas was delighted when he found a
picture of a tiger. He cut it out with great care and
pasted it next to the part of the picture that
represented a pool. At teatime the adults were duly
impressed, as I had intended them to be. I left to go
home.

I called in on Elsie on the way back. I told her
about the new job and she said: "Poor little mite! It
just goes to show that money isn't everything."

The cat was crying outside the door again when I
arrived tonight. I let him in and gave him some
bread and milk. He looks terrible. I shall have to
relent and buy him some protein. I find it ethically
unacceptable to kill one set of creatures to feed
another set of parasite pets. But this cat, I cannot
look him in the eyes — his are half-covered by a
grey membrane. Some of the hair on his chest is
falling out and he licks the pink skin. Evidently he
really does depend on me.

It is eleven o'clock and I have put the pet outside.
A phone call came from Pasquale only to say he is
tired and that he will come and see me tomorrow.

Day Thirty

How or why do we always end up in these messes?
Or rather why do I have to end up in such a mess?

I had wanted to spend the evening at home and
had told Pasquale that he would find me there. At
nine o'clock Janet and two other friends from the
pub called at the house. I was particularly pleased
to see them; I prefer uninvited social events. We
drank one bottle of red wine before they persuaded
me to go to the pub with them. I said no about four
times before I gave in and went, leaving a note for
Pasquale on the front door, thinking that he always
comes late anyway and I would be back by then. He
came just as we were leaving. He was quite polite to
all — that is, to the others — rather chilly to me. We
all went to the pub but Pasquale refused any drink,
he said that he had an appointment.

When he left, I went outside with him. I told him
that I had made a mistake, that I had really meant to
stay in but. . . . No, no, he had to go, he said, adding
that he would come back later. I was sure that he
was not coming back. I asked if I could call to see
him later and he told me not to. At closing time
Janet and four or five others were going to the wine
bar. I left them to it, saying I would go home. I went
instead to find Pasquale. From the street I could see
a light dimly visible through the curtains. I rang
the bell and he answered the door dressed only in
underpants. We went up to his room. He
apologized once or twice, saying he was sorry to
have ruined the party, and I repeated that it was not
a party, just a mistake — but *not* a bad one. I was a bit
tipsy, I asked him to kiss me. He did so minimally.
He explained that he intends to leave very early in
the morning to go to Rome and therefore had come

early to see me so that we could spend an hour or so together.

"Can I stay the night here?" I asked.

"Do as you like," he replied. "But if you stay, I shall sleep downstairs."

I insisted that he remain in the room and we got into bed, with him keeping right to the edge of the mattress. I hugged him but there was no response so I moved over to the far edge of the mattress on the other side. I made a determined effort to cry (by remembering my dog, who was killed by a car when I was fifteen — this always works) but he was unstirred by my muffled sobs. What I was doing was despicable; a few years earlier I would have genuinely been in tears for the doing of it.

In the dark I got up, dressed and left.

Now at midnight I sit here knowing that he will not come — he is going away. (Don Giovanni has had an easy win over the *femme fatale* in the third division.)

Day Thirty-One

Thank goodness for poor Nicholas. Despite my own miseries I care for his. Also he makes me aware of the positive things there are to be had just in an ordinary life here in London, in contradiction to my current negative life-style. Instead of studying some part of anything interesting or going out and joining in discussion or action — e.g. being political in a real sense — I sit here alone, against all my better judgements, and mope over a man. There have been other men. Next year, or the year after, there will be another.

The simplest things defeat me. I gave up smoking

four days ago, only to go back to it today; I quit my maudlin habit of drinking myself silly when alone, only at the first sign of crisis I am back to desperately sipping from my glass of plonk.

I will not make enquiries to learn if he is really out of the country. If he is really gone away, I will not see him. If he has not gone, or when he returns, he can come and see me if he wants to. This time I will insist that we be friends, not lovers. If I had carried the day when I first told him, I might by now be over these withdrawal symptoms, incidentally missing a few delicious moments. I hear those words about the cake and eating it; they seem a bit apt, except the cake is eating me. I have achieved one thing, one enduring detail (who would ask for more?) out of this whole sorry period of my life — a sort of friend: this notebook. The confusion is being recorded. It makes no more, or less sense to write it down, but that in itself is about as much sense as most things acquire.

Also I am trying to be honest with my pupil — no false jolly expectations. I just hope that in continuing to achieve day after day some knowledge that the world is full of people, animals, things — and that we too are a part of it, even its beauty, that he and I will achieve a peaceful and joyful acceptance of our own austere little selves. I trust him to help me.

It is half-past twelve and I must go to bed or else I will be tired tomorrow, and it is these simple facts that make progress (for the want of a better word) possible.

What a terrible, long, rambling load of junk in this entry!

Day Thirty-Two

I feel sad today, even bitter. If I cannot have him, I will have no one.

I went out shopping this morning and then visited Elsie. Now she suffers giddy spells, maybe from the new drugs her doctor has given her. The doctor has advised her to go on a diet but she is sure that she will not be able to stick to it. What she needs is the barrel treatment. A Yorkshire man in the pub once spoke of a farmer up North who had acquired a reputation as a worker of miracles for his patience and understanding with troublesome dogs. In fact, this farmer stroked and talked kindly to the dog for as long as its owner took to disappear down the farm track, whereupon the dog was popped under an upturned half-barrel together with a large bowl of water; after about a week, a lean and usually very obedient dog emerged.

Every day Nicholas adds an episode to his story. I have decided not to show it to his parents, especially since I know that they are thinking of taking him to a child psychiatrist. The story concerns a little boy who lives in the middle of a vast forest with his mother. He is his mother's sole support. This boy, Peter, can turn his hand to anything and has many resources at his disposal. Today he flew an aeroplane to bomb attackers who were coming through the forest. Yesterday with timber from the forest he constructed a large hut, filled it with chickens, then he smashed all the eggs. Nicholas always finishes each section quite abruptly, or so it seems to me. A moment comes when he tells me that he has finished that bit of the story; and we just have to wait for the next day to fill up his creative reservoir again. Words or pictures on the page do not seem to lead anywhere by logical sequence — it all comes from within.

At the end of lessons today Mr and Mrs Philips asked me to stay behind and offered a drink as well. I accepted (a large Scotch). They said how pleased they are with Nicholas's progress and how much he likes his teacher. I was very pleased. Mrs Philips wondered if I might consider staying in the flat one weekend so that the two of them could go away together. I agreed, thinking it could be quite pleasant, a free holiday — rather better than free, because I would have money for it. They said that, of course, they did not want to spoil my social life and that I was welcome to invite one or two people to supper during my stay. I thanked them. Then, rather embarrassed, Mrs Philips asked if I could possibly stay this weekend; she had obviously thought that I might refuse, but I said yes. Everyone seemed pleased so, of course, we had another drink (a large Scotch).

Tonight I packed an overnight bag. Tomorrow I will buy some worthwhile new books. Probably I will end up watching colour TV (with a large Scotch).

Day Thirty-Three

In splendid comfort. I occupy one end of the downy sofa. Nicholas is already in bed. Two programmes have gone by on the television. For supper we ate sausages and mashed potatoes, Nicholas said that I was a good cook. I suggested that he could cook tomorrow and he told me that he has always wanted to make a cake.

We walked in the park today, inspecting the first tinges of autumn. We ate lunch in the Serpentine restaurant. The spacious setting, on a lawn overlooking the lake, gave us a feeling of isolated luxury. I had a "Salad Ethel" (limp lettuce daintied up with slices of beetroot and tomato). Nicholas ate a re-heated factory pork pie.

During lunch, without preamble, Nicholas recalled: "One night when we lived with my real mother," his younger brother has stayed with the mother, "we came in late and we all got undressed and huddled up together in her big bed." It was his memory of a moment of definitive warmth and comfort. For me there is a flashback to a lost past, when I saw a baby tucked up snug under the hood of a big old-fashioned pram; I must have been about three years old at the time.

Half of today we were wandering around the Natural History Museum. I feel I have fallen on my feet to get paid for doing this. I am now sipping my drink (a large Scotch), I reflect on the surroundings. I could easily wish that this were my flat. I seem to walk about here in a different way, through these wide spaces, with so many more steps before I hit a wall. The air is evenly warm, so that I find it pleasant, even late at night, to walk about without shoes.

I bought two new books but I have spent my reading time with a book of Mr Philips. The study is next to their own bedroom, white-carpeted, with an antique four-poster bed covered in a lace bedspread. The study has a spare bed where I am to sleep. Before sleeping, I shall read some more of a biography of John Stuart Mill.

Day Thirty-Four

Ten-thirty and Nicholas is still up, watching a televised football match. As though there were something rather grand about it, he explained that he has never been to a school where they played soccer. He also told me that he has to be in bed by nine o'clock. When the time came he obviously did not want to go and I did not really see any reason why I should insist. He is a funny little boy. When today I fancied some tea, he asked me: "Do you like Earl Grey? It costs 45p a quarter." It is a blend that may turn out to be my favourite; I shall buy myself some, despite the high cost! I have been left with a credit card for Harrods. I refused the car, not wishing to test my luck so soon again. The use of this flat with a fridge full of goodies and a cupboard full of multi-hued booze, all a nice bonus to the job of watching over Nicholas, whose company I enjoy so much that I would care for him out of my own pocket, if I had to.

I feel very calm and contented. Maybe the difficulties of my life's problems were only worth a few thousand pounds, after all. I will help myself to a tiny night-cap (a large Scotch).

Nicholas is a bit sleepy, although he is still trying to take an interest in the box. Soon we shall go to bed.

Day Thirty-Six

Back in my austere room I feel a bit shaky, rather too strange to go to bed yet. I do not know whether to regret or feel good about how things have turned out.

Yesterday morning, in the glory of a summer's day, Nicholas and I ran through the park. We stopped to gaze at the exhibition in the Serpentine Gallery where I launched into an explanation about art being anything of beauty performed with care, that links people to some ideal. I do not think that he listened much, but he did look at the exhibits, which included fairly ordinary photographs and texts about working conditions in coal mines. I want to avoid any direct influence over his thoughts — I only wish to make things and ideas available to him. We ate a caterer's approximation of an English Sunday lunch at the restaurant, I regretted the heavy feeling that followed. We returned to the flat and read some Sunday papers. After tea we took a bus to the West End to see a Western with Clint Eastwood in a passion of destruction that paralleled the fictitious boy, Peter. In common with the rest of the audience, we found the entertainment both frightening and exciting. Afterwards Nicholas pronounced it the best film he had ever seen. He also knew that it was a good film because it must have cost a lot of money to make!

When we got back his father was in the flat, standing in the hall in a tweed jacket, cavalry twill trousers and slippers, with a glass of whisky in his hand. His wife has stayed in the country until the next day. I said that I would leave. He asked us what we had been doing and whether we had had supper yet. It was gratifying that Nicholas enthusiastically launched into a lengthy and accurate description of our doings. Mr Philips smiled with pleasure at his happy and articulate son. I said that we had eaten a big lunch and I was not really hungry. Mr Philips was not hungry either, but it appeared there was a good restaurant nearby where we could have just a light meal. I sat in the front, Nicholas in the back, in the big Mercedes. We drew up in front of a restaurant I knew by name to be both famous and very expensive; this was the "little place close by". I entered very calmly, assured of my role; I had cast myself as Jane Eyre. This was a restaurant where, for a mass of money, you can pick delicate items to eat without ever feeling full. I had a fish cocktail and then salad, Nicholas had steak and chips, while Mr Philips toyed with a piece of sole in white sauce. We drank a marvellous white Burgundy and — an impressive touch of elegance — we also had a bottle of sparkling mineral water, probably costing as much as I would normally pay for wine. It is quite an art eating when you are not hungry.

I would be quite good at being rich, I realized, because I am good at being poor. As we were driven back to the flat I just felt good altogether, and after Nicholas was sent to bed said yes please to a small night-cap before being taken home (six massive whiskies).

"I see that you are reading John Stuart Mill," Mr Philips remarked. "He used to be a hero of mine."

"I have reservations about him. Didn't he quell the revolutionary spirit of the times? I find myself torn between the revolutionary spirit and the liberal."

We talked on and on, the whisky inducing both eloquence and a convivial feeling about English history. Mr Philips (Angus) waxed enthusiastic about the transformation I am believed to have wrought in his son. It all seemed very momentous and very grand. When he kissed me, that too was inevitable, and after we had made love in a friendly, hopelessly drunken way, on the sofa, he said that he loved his wife and that he hoped that I understood that, I said that I was glad. I said that I

would rather go home than spend the rest of the
night there, and persuaded him to ring for a taxi,
although he wanted to drive me. He left me with
ten pounds for the cab, which cost three pounds
fifty. Tomorrow it will all be a warm harmless
memory.

I suppose I am one of the family now.

Day Thirty-Seven

Ten p.m. I have just woken up. I got into bed as soon
as I came in this evening. During lessons I was so
tired that I rather left Nicholas on his own. We had
lunch in a Wimpy Bar and then went to the park. I
snoozed on a bench while Nicholas collected as
many different types of leaves as he could find. On
the way back to the flat we bought a book about
trees. His step-mother was there when we
returned. He seemed to avoid her kiss, I thought. I
left soon afterwards leaving him to identify as
many of the leaves as possible before tomorrow, as
homework. He looked a bit crestfallen and I felt a
twinge of disloyalty towards him. My first and only
loyalty will be to that child.

A phone call for me. Pasquale is back; he only
went to Brussels, it seems. He will be round in ten
minutes' time. He rang to see if he should call.

Day Thirty-Eight

It is only nine o'clock but it seems like midnight.

Last night Pasquale arrived with a bottle of
Dutch gin. He left the bottle on the table with his

holdall open beside it while he went downstairs to fetch some glasses. I thought I would take a look at the photograph in his Italian passport that was lying on top of some of his clothes. As I opened the booklet a newspaper cutting fell out, headed, as I recollect: GANG OF ITALIANS SET UP BUSINESS AS CAR DESTROYERS. The report went on to explain how a gang of unemployed Italians resident in England had provided a permanent disposal service for motor vehicles in order to defraud insurance companies. I was reading this scrap of paper when Pasquale came in and snatched it from me.

"It has nothing to do with me. I thought I might know one of them, that's all!" he said. He put the cutting back into his passport.

"Let me see it again," I demanded, but instead he handed me a glass of gin, oily on ice. He asked me if I had missed him, then so many questions followed that I understood he was anxious to avoid any further questions from me. We kissed and went to bed. It all seemed very neutral, he sensed my detachment and said that I no longer loved him, indeed that I had never loved him — I had only said the words. I almost shouted "thank you". After that he apologized with the excuse that, although he knew he was being difficult, things had been very bad for him but that now it would all become better.

It was two o'clock when he left to go back to his room in order to be there early in the morning to pay rent to the Italian architect before he left to go to the office. I asked him if he had enough money. He had enough he replied, and, anyway, he did not accept money from women. Then he kissed me fondly.

Tomorrow Pasquale is eating with his family; the day after tomorrow he is coming to take me out to dinner.

Day Thirty-Nine

My wardrobe had been flung open and most of my clothes strewn about the floor. My mouth was opening in amazement as I turned to see my black stockings over the chair back and Pasquale standing, stiff with rage, beside the bed. He put one hand on my shoulder and hit me hard across the face with the other.

"You told me you had lost the key!" I managed to blurt out, realizing it was an inadequate response to all this.

He hit me with his other hand. This does not hurt as much as I thought it might. I was anxious for him not to break my teeth. Inwardly I felt very calm — I had to take charge to overcome the confusion. Underneath the table I saw the immediate cause for this outrage: the pages of the notebook — my diary — were torn out and scattered over the floor. One sheet remained on the table. He picked it up and fanned with it to hit my face. I turned my head away. He screwed the paper up and threw it at me.

"'Made love in a drunken hopeless way' — eh? Why don't you go back to your rich lover, you whore! Come on!" He pulled at my arm until it hurt. "Come on, I want to see him. I'm going to kill you both. I know where he lives, come on!" He tried to drag me through the door. I managed to free myself and got back into the room. He followed and slammed the door closed.

I sat on the bed. I was still calm. I wondered if he really did know the Philips' address. I did not think so.

"Pasquale. Please sit down. Listen to me, I'm sorry. It isn't that important really. . . ."

He ripped away at my shirt.

"Stop it," I said. "Listen to me, please."

He shoved me backwards so my head hit the wall as I fell back on to the bed. He was pulling my clothes off and pummelling me to the left and the right. I saw that he had an erection. I felt a sense of superior disgust. I gave up resistance while he pulled his trousers off and pulled my legs over his shoulders to ram into me. He hit me again and again around the face. He sobbed out that I was a whore. He said that he was going to kill me. I felt sorry for him. I was otherwise determined to feel nothing. He turned me over and fucked me from behind, he buggered me, which was painful as usual. I tried to show nothing, but to his evident satisfaction I could not stay silent when it hurt so much. I was put on my back for the finale. When he had come he stuck his hand into my vagina and then rubbed it, all wet over my face, but the intensity, the force, was gone.

He gazed down at his own body, got off the bed, pulled up and fastened his trousers. Then he sat in the chair with his head in his hands. Even then I felt I might go and comfort him, but I knew it was better not to touch him. I gathered the bedclothes up to cover myself. My jaw was beginning to ache and, feeling wet tears on my cheeks, I did not know if I was crying for fear or for relief.

The next thing I remember was waking up with him shaking me by the shoulders, he was calling, "Katie, Katie."

When I opened my eyes I moved away from him quickly.

He came quietly to sit on the edge of the bed beside me. "I thought that you were dead."

I almost laughed — he looked so worried, the

would-be killer — but I still had a lot of fear. I remembered everything that had happened and I wanted to remain silently, cautiously in command.

"Why did you just stand there and let me hit you?"

I had no answer. I wanted him to go away but realized that I should encourage him to stay because I was more afraid that he would go to the Philips' house than of what he might do to me. I asked for some water and he came with a milk bottle full. We drank gin and water like a silent toast to a mutual realization that we were finally separated.

I went to the mirror. My face was already swollen, the right eye red, about to turn black, blood was drying around my nose. When I moved, my body was painful. I covered myself with a woollen sweater and an elastic-waisted skirt that came down to my ankles; I felt almost cosy, like a child dressed after swimming. The cat was crying on the windowsill outside, visible through the partly drawn curtains, it was nearly dark. I put on the light and sat on the bed.

Pasquale murmured apologies. I did not reply.

The page lay on the floor, the honest mistake, the crumpled detail that decided the end. The power of the written word. Why had I bothered to write this diary?

We sat and sipped our drinks in silence.

I shall never write a diary again.